KT-157-742

KNIGHT SIR LOUIS

AND THE SORCERER OF SLIME

by The Brothers McLeod

GUPPY BOOKS

KNIGHT SIR LOUIS AND THE SORCERER OF SLIME!
is a GUPPY BOOK

First published in 2022 by
Guppy Books,
Bracken Hill,
Cotswold Road,
Oxford OX2 9JG

Text copyright © The Brothers McLeod

978 1 913101 688

1 3 5 7 9 10 8 6 4 2

The rights of The Brothers McLeod to be identified as
the author of this work has been asserted in accordance
with the Copyright, Designs and Patents Act 1988.

All rights reserved. No part of this publication may be reproduced,
stored in a retrieval system, or transmitted in any form or by
any means, electronic, mechanical, photocopying, recording or
otherwise, without the prior permissions of the publishers.

Papers used by Guppy Books are from well-managed
forests and other responsible sources.

MIX
Paper from
responsible sources
FSC® C171272

GUPPY PUBLISHING LTD Reg. No. 11565833

A CIP catalogue record for this book is
available from the British Library.

Typeset in 13½/20 pt Adobe Garamond by
Falcon Oast Graphic Art Ltd, www.falcon.uk.com

Printed and bound in Great Britain by CPI Books Ltd

For Louis, Lyla, Audrey and Finty

SO WHO'S IN THIS

The young hero of this tale. A calm and clear-thinking champion in a bonkers world. All the most difficult quests are entrusted to him. His name is pronounced 'Loo-ee'.

CLUNKALOT

The trusty mechanical steed. Sturdy, brave and always ready to join his beloved master Louis on a dangerous quest. Also loves flying and poetry.

OOK EXACTLY?

READER CATALOGUE

One of Louis' best friends. She's a super-smart boar with a degree in Weird Botany.

PEARLIN

A young, self-taught wizard and inventor (or wizentor!). Always coming up with new and fun ways of using machines and magic.

KING BURT THE NOT BAD

The (mostly) kind and (usually) fair King of Squirrel Helm who lives in Castle Sideways.

DAVE THE SWORD

A magical sword recycled from a magic mirror. Likes reflecting magical spells, chopping up nasty things and singing. (Is an awful singer.)

MAC N CHEESE

Pearlin's pet dragon with two (fortunately friendly) heads. Growing rapidly!

SQUIRE LYME

Louis' new apprentice knight. A handsome, dashing hero. Loves handing out tasty gummies.

WURT

A young, small forest ogre who writes books (even though it's not allowed).

MYSTO

The greatest wizentor ever known. Prone to magical accidents.

HAGATHA SQUINT

An apprentice witch with one big ambition. TO LIVE FOREVER! HAHAHAHAHAHA!

ACIDIC ALAN

A cunning and gooey master of slime magic. Ugh!

CHAPTER 1

Hello?

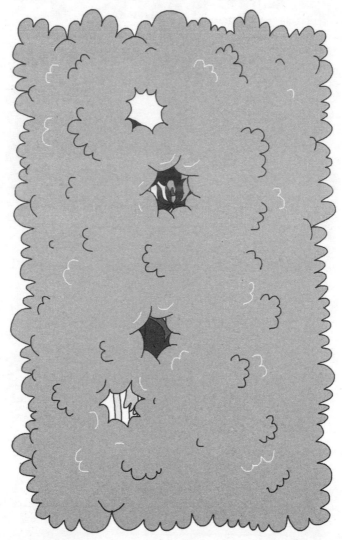

Hellooooo?

Why is it so foggy? Books aren't supposed to start like this, you know.

Oh, wait a minute. Something's happening.

Starting to clear, now. That's good. Soon we'll be able to see . . .

Gulp! Let's do Chapter 1 again. And as fast we can!

CHAPTER 1 AGAIN

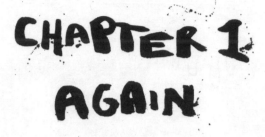

Hello?

Helloooo?

What's going on this time?

What's that slopping over the page?

Ugh. It's slime! Yuck!

QUICK! Change chapters again!

CHAPTER 2

Well, what a ridiculous way to start a book! Let's hope this chapter has some knights and castles in it.

Here's Knight Sir Louis, the champion knight at Castle Sideways in the land of Squirrel Helm. Sounds most impressive, doesn't it?

RIGHT.

BUT THAT'S NOT ALL.

HE DOES LOADS OF STUFF.

Quite right. He's also:

THE SCROLL OF KNIGHT SIR LOUIS' MANY ACHIEVEMENTS

- Deputy King
- Slayer of Evil Dragons with Brains in their Bottom
- Defeater of Naughty Wizards
- Defender against Evil Potatoes
- Wielder of rare Ice Cucumbers
- Thinker of Great Plans (Grade 9)
- Piano (Grade 1)
- Robot Horse Engineer (Level 1)
- Maker of Omelettes (Level 5)
- Eater of Puddings (Level 10)

And he's just about to finish his latest mission. Let's see what that is . . .

Castle Sideways was under attack. A hoard of armoured gnomes from the southlands of Snoozin-by-the-Pond had come to claim the castle and the land of Squirrel Helm. The gnomes were fierce. The gnomes were many. The gnomes were noisy.

ARRARRRGEFOOOO!

If we translate that from gnome language, it means:

ARRARRRGEFOOOO!

. . . because, you know, it's more of a war cry than an actual word.

Luckily for everyone in the castle, Pearlin the wizard and inventor (or wizentor) had recently installed an alarm system – a very noisy gargoyle that lived on top of the castle. She called it the

Klaxongoyle. Here she is receiving first prize at the Wizentor's Conference for Best Invention of the Year.

YEAR OF OUR LLAMA 802
PEARLIN WINS WITH
ALARMING INVENTION

The Klaxongoyle spotted the oncoming gnomes and shouted:

Oi! You lot! There's a bunch of gnomes coming! Watch out! Oi! You listenin' to me? Wake up, you lazy bunch! Cor blimey!

CHAPTER 3

A moment later, Knight Sir Louis was out of bed and ready for action. He could have stayed in his pyjamas if he'd wanted to, because they are also made of armour.

He grabbed his magic sword Dave (full name: Senator Jibber Jabber Ticket Flick It Sprocket

Wicket Dingle David) and jumped onto his brave robot horse, Clunkalot.

They flew out to meet the gnomes in battle. The marauding gnomes saw Louis flying in. They raised their fishing rods and flicked them towards Louis.

DON'T INVADERS USUALLY USE SWORDS?

OR SPEARS?

YEAH. BUT GNOMES LOVE A BIT OF FISHING.

THEY'RE GOOD AT IT TOO! WATCH OUT LOUIS!

Fishing lines and fishing hooks shot towards Louis. Oh no! But he pulled on Clunkalot's reins, sending him into a spiral. They whirled round and round and Louis swished and swashed with his sword, slicing through the fishing lines.

Then Clunkie flew down in front of the gnomes and Louis jumped down to face them. The leading gnome stood forward.

'Listen to me! I am General Gnomus,' he said. 'Give up your land to us or we will take it from you.'

'I don't think so,' said Louis.

'You will so,' said the general. 'And when we do, we will turn this land into a beautiful garden with flowers and ponds. Lots of ponds. With fish. And beside the ponds there'll be lots of stone toadstools to sit on . . . SO BE AFRAID!'

'That sounds quite nice,' said Louis. 'We could do with someone to help us with the castle garden.'

'Don't mock me,' said the general. 'Though we would do a very good job of that. You have too many weeds here. Anyway, LISTEN! Give up while you can. You don't stand a chance against us. There's loads of us and only one of you.'

'Yes,' said Louis. 'That's true. But . . . I'm also twenty times bigger.'

'That doesn't bother us,' said the general. 'We'll still defeat you.'

'Also,' said Louis, 'I'm not really alone.'

He pointed upwards. Pearlin was flying in on her double-headed dragon, Mac n Cheese, who were firing from both heads as they approached. (Dragons had never made it to Snoozin-By-The-Pond. As a result, gnomes thought dragons were just a fairy story. Until now.)

The gnomes, very sensibly, panicked.

ARRARRRGEFOOOO!

'We'll all be toasted!' wailed the general.

'Why don't you hide inside Clunkalot?' suggested Louis. He pointed to his robot horse. A hatch opened on the side and the gnomes ran in without a second thought. As the last one jumped inside, the hatch closed.

'Gotcha,' said Louis to himself.

Pearlin and Mac n Cheese came in to land.

'Need any help?' she asked.

'You already helped,' said Louis. He patted the dragon on both heads.

When Pearlin first adopted Mac n Cheese from the land of Doooooom, they were about the size of a dog, but now they were as big as a horse! It wasn't a very comfy ride, since their back was a bit knobbly, but it was very warm thanks to all the dragon fire stored inside.

'Come on,' said Louis. 'Let's get back to the castle. I want to know why gnomes are attacking Squirrel Helm.'

CHAPTER 4

King Burt the Not Bad was excited. He had just received a brand-new computer game – *Hedgepig Herk Noodle and the Poodles of Doom*. He unboxed the game, turned on his computer (a PlayFortress XS) and loaded the game. At that exact moment, the Klaxongoyle screamed its warning.

'NOT NOW!' shouted King Burt.

A short while later, Knight Sir Louis arrived in the Great Hall in Castle Sideways to stand before the king. King Burt paced up and down.

'What's happened? It's not going to take long, is it? I've got a new game to play!'

'We stopped an invasion of gnomes, your majesty,' said Louis.

'Who cares!' said King Burt.

'I thought we should find out why they were invading,' said Louis. 'I thought you might like to know too?'

'Who cares! Who cares!' said King Burt, desperate to play his game.

He strode up to Louis and said, 'You know your trouble, Sir Louis? You're always interrupting things. Battles here. Battles there.'

'I'm just trying to defend the realm, sir,' said Louis, feeling a bit upset and confused.

'I don't need to know why a bunch of gnomes are here,' said King Burt. 'You sort it out. I've got some very important games to play!'

'But, sir—'

'No buts!' said King Burt. 'In fact, I order you to play my new game with me now, two-player mode. No arguments.'

'Yes, your majesty,' said Louis obediently.

King Burt was thrilled to finally play his new game. Louis decided to do as he was told, but finish the game as quickly as possible. Then he could get back to finding out why the gnomes had invaded. But things didn't work out as he planned.

Usually, King Burt was much better than Louis at computer games, but this was a game of strategy. You had to find clues and uncover secrets and escape from dangerous situations. It was right up Louis' street. He was a natural. He thrashed the king easily. When he'd won, he turned to King Burt and smiled. 'Shall we see the gnomes now, sir?'

But King Burt was not smiling. He was very annoyed to have lost so badly.

'NO!' he barked. 'I want another go. You fluked that win.'

Louis shrugged and they played again. This time Louis beat the king even more quickly.

'AGAIN!' said King Burt. 'You were lucky . . . twice. That's all!'

Before they could play a third round, the Klaxongoyle burst into life again.

Oi! You LOT!
THERE'S SOMETHING COMING!
WATCH OUT! WAKE UP YOU
LAZY LOT - OH HANG ON!
THERE'S ONLY ONE OF 'EM.
COULD BE A FRIEND?
BETTER BE CAREFUL
THOUGH.
BETTER TO
BE SAFE THAN
SORRY AND
ALL THAT!

Knight Sir Louis raced to the window and looked out. This time, it wasn't an invasion, unless you can call one person an invasion.

'Don't worry, your majesty, I'll find out who he is and what he wants,' said Louis and he rushed off to find Clunkalot.

'Whatever,' said King Burt. 'Just find me someone else to play with! Someone fun!' And he switched off his computer game and had a really big sulk in the corner.

CHAPTER 5

Knight Sir Louis arrived at the castle gates as the visitor strode up the path. He was a young man with flowing locks of hair, a handsome uniform, and the greenest eyes you've ever seen.

The castle courtiers had also heard the Klaxongoyle and came to see the visitor. They had been afraid of another gnome attack, but now they saw the young man and started muttering to one another.

And you know what that means don't you?

No. Of course not.

And neither do I.

Because we can't really hear what they're saying.

Let's get closer.

Louis held up a gauntlet to stop him and said, 'Morning, stranger. Welcome to Castle Sideways. How can we help you?'

The young man looked at Louis in wonder.

'Be you Louis?' he asked.

'Yes. I . . . be Louis.'

'Oh, really?' said the man. 'You're a lot younger than I thought.'

'Is that a problem?' asked Louis. He wondered if this visitor was one of those adults that say things like . . .

- CHILDREN SHOULD BE SEEN AND NOT HEARD.
- GIVE ME A BITE OF YOUR ICE CREAM.
- IF YOU DON'T PICK UP YOUR THINGS I'M GOING TO THROW THEM AWAY.
- GOLD COINS DON'T GROW ON TREES, YOU KNOW!
- DO YOU WANT ME TO TURN THIS CART AROUND, RIGHT NOW?
- SWEETS AREN'T GOOD FOR YOU. HAVE THIS RAW CABBAGE INSTEAD.

But then the young man said, 'No matter! If you are Louis, then my journey is at an end. I come to warn you that a great enemy is preparing to attack the land of Squirrel Helm.'

'If it's gnomes, then we've already sorted that,' said Louis.

'Not gnomes,' said the young man, 'but the Wild Forest Ogres of Tumblin' Klatterbang!'

'Ogres?' said Louis. 'Why would ogres want to attack us?'

'I know not,' said the young man, 'but I humbly offer my services to you. My name is Squire Lyme!'

He dropped to his knees and dipped his head.

GREAT! A SQUIRE FOR LOUIS!

GOOD NEWS. A SQUIRE.

YEAH. BRILLIANT. THE BEST... ER... WHAT'S A SQUIRE?

SQUIRE SQUARE'S
SQUIRE GUIDE

Hi! I'm Squire Square and I'm here to squanswer all your squestions about squiring.

What is a squire?
A squire is a trainee knight!

How do you become a squire?
First of all, find a knight willing to train you.

What do you do when you're a squire?

You will learn lots of new skills. For example . . . looking after a knight's armour! Like this:

Help your knight remove their armour.

Wash your knight's armour.

Fix your knight's armour.

Polish your knight's armour.

Get told off for not polishing your knight's armour well enough.

Polish your knight's armour some more.

Get told off again.

Polish some more.

At last . . .

Help your knight put their armour back on.

(Do it all again, next day!)

After a while you can move onto more advanced lessons (some with badges!) like:

The Fighting Evil-doers Badge!
The Horse Riding Badge!
The Riding on Giant Flying Hamster Badge!
(Yes, really!)
The Posing like a Hero Badge!

Eventually you'll know enough to become a knight yourself!
Wow!
Then you can get your own squire!
Go for it!

This guide is published by Obadiah Haywire in Fire Shire.

CHAPTER 6

'This is turning out to be a very busy day,' thought Knight Sir Louis. He'd captured some gnomes, heard about an ogre attack, and acquired a squire!

He wasn't really sure he wanted a squire, but it sounded like they might need all the help they could get if Squire Lyme was right about these ogres. There were a lot of questions to ask and he wasn't sure where to start. Louis remembered his mother's wise words.

IF YOU WANT TO INVENT THE WHEEL... HAVE A MEAL

So, Louis took Squire Lyme to lunch.

Louis welcomed Squire Lyme to the Great Hall. Lyme was thrilled to meet everyone. He made a great impression on the courtiers.

It was true that Squire Lyme did have a very impressive smile. His teeth twinkled when he smiled. But not as much as his green eyes. They twinkled even more.

Squire Lyme was also thrilled when Louis introduced him to Clunkalot.

 'Oh Clunkalot. The famous Clunkie! What a lovely robot horsey!' said the squire. He pulled a bright green sweet from a paper bag and offered it up. 'Here! Have a gummy!'

Clunkalot didn't really eat food, but he swallowed it anyway to be polite.

'And, oh, what a lovely dragon,' said Squire Lyme when he saw Mac n Cheese. 'I suppose you want a gummy too?' he said with a big smile.

Mac n Cheese didn't need to be offered twice. They snaffled down the whole bag of gummies.

'Ah no! Sorry!' said Pearlin. 'They're big eaters. Always gobbling down anything. Still growing, you see!'

'Oh, I don't mind,' said Lyme with that huge smile again. 'I'm thrilled they like them so much. Wonderful. Just wonderful!'

King Burt came stomping down from his rooms into the Great Hall, following the smell of cooking.

'I say,' he said, 'why did no one tell me it was lunchtime! And Sir Louis! Didn't I tell you to find me someone to play with? Well? Well?'

In all the excitement, Louis had completely forgotten. Before he could reply, Squire Lyme had thrown himself down flat on the ground in front of King Burt.

'OH, YOUR MAJESTY KING BURT THE BRILLIANT! I AM YOUR HUMBLE SQUIRE

LYME! LET ME BE THE ONE TO HELP YOU IN YOUR HOUR OF NEED! THOUGH I AM NOT FIT TO LICK YOUR BOOTS CLEAN, LET ME HELP! OH, YOUR MAJESTY KING BURT THE BEST BOSS EVER!'

'I'm very sorry,' said Louis rushing over, 'this is our new visitor and—'

'AND he's very welcome,' said King Burt. He much preferred being called brilliant and best boss ever, instead of 'not bad'.

'Humble Squire Lyme, come and play my new game,' said the king. Then he turned to Louis,

'And you can bring us up some sandwiches.'

'BUT—' said Louis, who had more important things to sort out.

'NO BUTS!' said the king, and he was gone, back upstairs with Squire Lyme.

CHAPTER 7

Knight Sir Louis went to make a royal sandwich for the king (stinky blue cheese and extra strong pickle). He'd only just started spreading the butter on the bread when the Klaxongoyle started screaming for the third time that day!

WHOA! OiOi!
THERE'S A WITCH FLYING IN!
WATCH OUT!
Oi! YOU LISTENIN TO ME?
WAKE UP YOU LAZY BUNCH!
COR BLIMEY!

Pearlin peered out of the window. Sure enough someone was flying in on a broomstick. Pearlin reached into her pocket and pulled out her small telescope.

Here's what she expected to see.

AHA HA HA
HA HA HA
HA HA
HA H

But what she actually saw was . . .

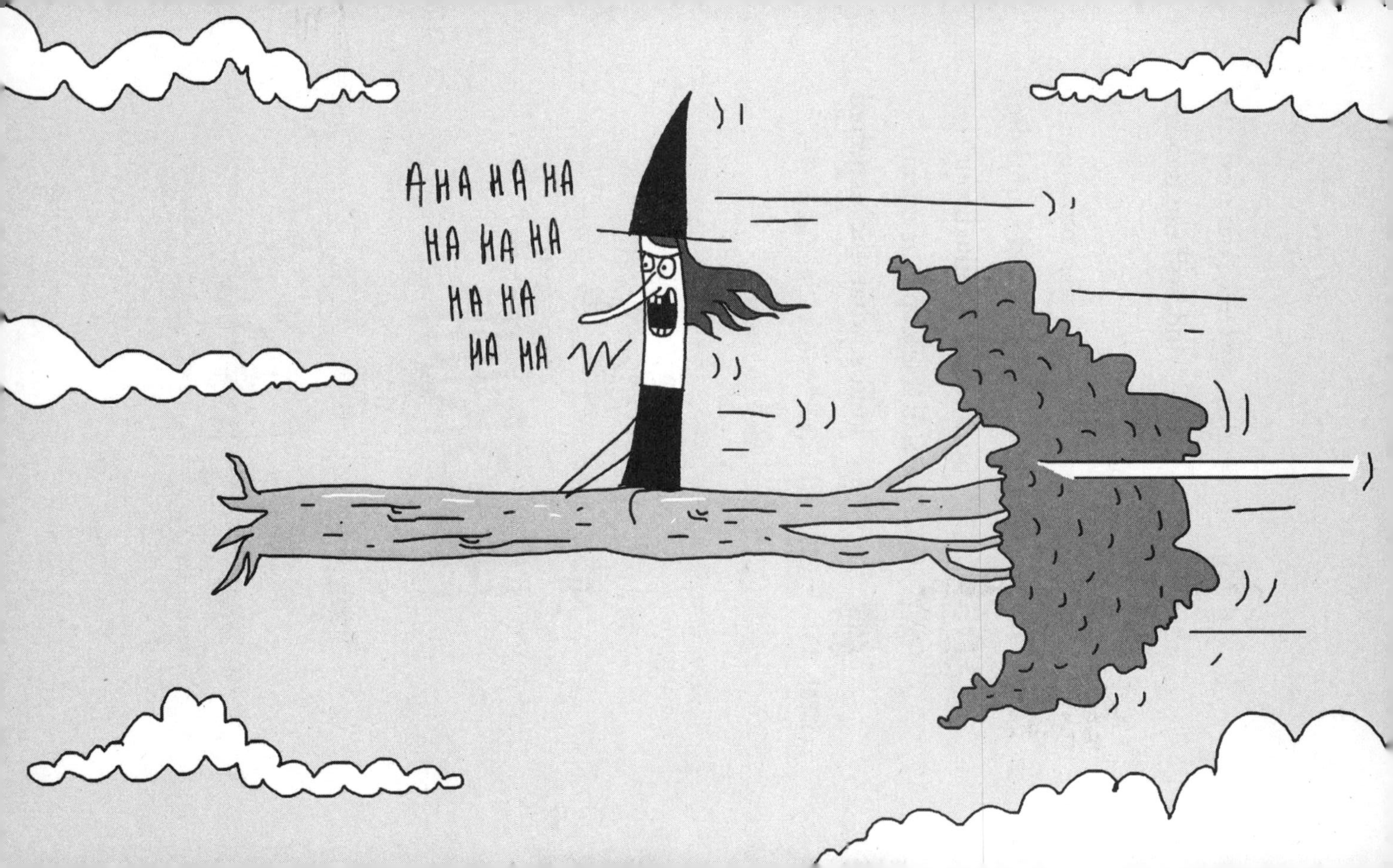
AHA HA HA
HA HA HA
HA HA
HA HA

'It's a witch riding in on a MASSIVE tree!'

Louis rushed to Pearlin's side, still holding his half-made sandwich.

'Not something you see every day,' he said.

'Friend or enemy, do you think?' asked Pearlin.

'Do your friends usually fly at you with trees?'

'Good point!' she said. 'Let's assume enemy!'

Knight Sir Louis jumped onto Clunkalot's back. Pearlin leaped onto Mac n Cheese.

'LET'S FLY!' they said in unison.

The courtiers cheered.

HOORAH!

Clunkalot and Mac n Cheese leaped out of the window . . .

. . . and plummeted straight down towards the ground.

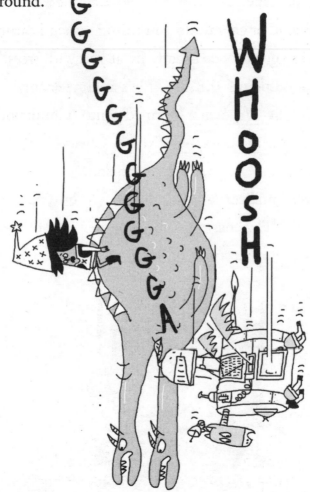

Oh dear! Let's take a closer look at Clunkalot and Mac n Cheese.

Clunkalot's wings were struggling to unfurl. They seemed to be covered in a nasty green goo. Where had that come from?

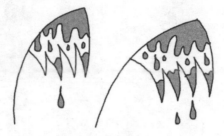

Mac n Cheese felt very heavy and burped mid-air. BURP! A nasty green slime flew out of their mouths and nostrils.

Hmm! Interesting! What's going on with all that slime?

Back to the action . . .

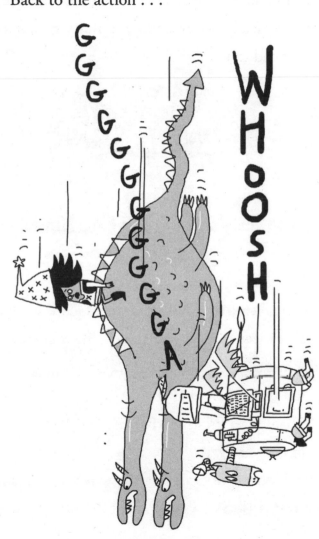

Luckily, Knight Sir Louis had recently recommended that Castle Sideways install a moat around the hill. The builders had finished digging the hole the day before and were filling it up with water.

Louis, Pearlin, Clunkie and Mac n Cheese floated to the surface and pulled themselves out of the moat.

'Plan B!' said Louis.

'What's plan B?' asked Pearlin.

'I'm not sure yet!'

They looked up and saw the witch still racing towards Castle Sideways on her flying tree.

'BOOM!'
THWACK!

The tree rammed into the castle, smashing a hole in the wall to the Great Hall. It hurled the witch inside.

'I think whatever Plan B is, it's going to happen inside . . .' said Louis, and they all raced back into the castle.

CHAPTER 8

Meanwhile, King Burt had been playing his new computer game with Squire Lyme. The king had started enjoying himself, because Squire Lyme was so useless at playing. King Burt had won every game so far.

'You really are the best, your majesty,' said Lyme. 'I really don't know how you do it.'

'Believe it not, Sir Louis was even better than me,' said King Burt

'Oh surely not, sir,' said Lyme. 'Perhaps Sir Louis has played the game before?'

'You mean, he practised on his own first?' said the king.

'Could be,' said Lyme with a sparkle in his green eyes.

'But that would be like . . . cheating!' said King Burt.

'Oh, I'm sure Knight Sir Louis isn't a cheating-cheaty-cheater,' said the squire with one of his large grins. 'No sir. Though, of course, he is still a child. A mere boy. And children can't be trusted, can they?'

Just then the Klaxongoyle sounded, and shortly after there was a huge crash as a flying tree hit the castle.

'What the blazes?!' said the king.

'To the rescue!' said Squire Lyme. He jumped up and ran down to the Great Hall, with King Burt a short way behind him.

The witch stood in the Great Hall. She looked like a classic witch. Very old. Long grey hair. Big black hat. Strange curvy nose. Some warts. She was shooting bolts of blue magic from two wands. The courtiers hid from her under the dining table.

She was cackling and shouting: 'Tremble! For Hagatha Squint is here! And I will turn you all into toads!'

ZAP!

Squire Lyme raced forward bravely. He rushed past the table where lunch had been set out. He grabbed a bowl of hummus and plopped it on his head. It made an effective helmet. The hummus helped it stick, plus some of it dripped down into Lyme's mouth

– an excellent snack while fighting off baddies. He picked up a silver plate as a shield and a long baguette as a sword.

'Prepare for battle, foul witch!' said Lyme.

The king was impressed. 'What a hero!' he said.

The courtiers were impressed too. 'He's so dashing! Even in hummus.'

Hagatha fired off some bolts of magic from her wands. Lyme deflected them with his silver plate and leaped forward and broke his baguette over her head.

'Oh woe is me,' she said loudly, as though reading from a script. 'I am defeated. Bread is like poison to me. Woe. Woe. How did you know? Oh no. Oh no. And now I fall over and can be taken to your dungeon. Ugh.'

Then she dropped her wands and fell to the floor.

The king and the courtiers jumped about for joy.

51

'HOORAH FOR SQUIRE LYME.'

Just then, Knight Sir Louis and Pearlin raced back into the Great Hall. They saw the witch lying on the floor and the courtiers carrying Squire Lyme around like a hero.

'Oh, there you are,' said the king to Louis and Pearlin. He looked very unimpressed with them. 'Lucky Squire Lyme was here. Not only is he a great hero, able to defeat witches with a simple baguette, but he also doesn't cheat at computer games.'

Sir Louis had a feeling in his toes. Also in his knees, elbows and little fingers. The feeling was saying this . . .

CHAPTER 9

It was late. Louis was tucked up in bed. What a strange day it had been. It was unusual for the Klaxongoyle to go off once, never mind three times in one day . . .

Suddenly, he remembered the gnomes! He hadn't let them out of Clunkalot. With the arrival of Squire Lyme and then Hagatha, he'd completely forgotten about them. He jumped out of bed and headed down to Pearlin's laboratory. She'd taken

Mac n Cheese and Clunkie back there after the flying slime incident.

What had caused that? wondered Louis.

Perhaps it was the gnomes' fault?

But they were only inside Clunkie. Not inside the dragon.

Then he remembered the gummies that Squire Lyme had given to Clunkalot and Mac n Cheese. Could that be it? The gummies were green, after all . . .

Louis was almost at the laboratory when he heard a strange noise. A slithering. A slopping. A glooping . . . It seemed to be coming from the stairwell that led down to the dungeons. Quietly,

Louis crept along the corridor to the stairs and made his way down.

It was very dark, but he heard a strange, wobbly voice say, 'I brought you something to eat.'

And then he heard Hagatha reply, 'Thank you master. Is it time now, master? Please can you turn me into a slimeball?' Her voice sounded different. Not like the typical witchy voice she'd used before. It sounded softer somehow.

'Patience,' said the wobbly voice. 'There is still work to do here. And besides, that annoying wizentor has put a holding spell on your cell. It won't be easy to undo.'

Louis stepped into the dungeon with a clang and lit one of the torches.

'Who's there?' he shouted.

But he could only see Hagatha Squint in her dungeon cell chewing on a sandwich. There was no one else. Though there was a strange green puddle of slime on the floor, seeping away through the cracks. Ugh!

Louis approached Hagatha.

'What's going on? Who were you talking to?' he asked.

'No one,' she said, with a mouthful of food.

'I know someone's been here because they brought you a sandwich.'

'No,' she said, chewing, 'I had this in my pocket all along.'

'Wait a minute!' said Louis. 'A sandwich! Made of bread! I thought bread was poison to you?'

She stopped chewing and looked worried. 'Er . . . it . . . er . . . was. But now I'm cured. Hooray!'

Louis came closer still, right up against the bars. Something wasn't quite right about Hagatha. Her hat had fallen back a little. Her grey hair had moved with it. It was a wig. And that strange, curved nose . . . it was held on with string. And at least one of her warts had fallen off.

'You're not a witch, are you?' he said and he poked at her hat. It fell off to reveal a shock of

short, spiky grey hair. She looked like a regular elderly lady.

'Fair enough, I'm not a witch,' she said defensively. 'Not yet. I'm an apprentice, all right? Been in training for years. Years and years. Any moment now, I'm going to be made a full witch. Any moment. Soon. Maybe tomorrow. Or next week. Or sometime in the next few years. Aw!'

'So, who's training you? Who's your master?'

But Hagatha refused to say. She just sat down, sulked and ate her sandwich.

Knight Sir Louis' funny feelings spoke up again.

Louis raced up out of the dungeons and along to the guest chamber. He opened the door and found Squire Lyme sleeping soundly in a bunk bed, a wide grin on his face. His teeth twinkled in the moonlight.

There was nothing suspicious to see, so Louis retreated.

But as he closed the door, he thought for a
moment he saw something in the half-light. It
looked like a blob of green slime seeping up out
of the ground, sliding up into Squire Lyme's bed.

Louis rushed back in, shouting, 'Watch out,
Squire Lyme!'

Squire Lyme shrieked with surprise. 'What!
Oh! Ah! Sir Louis?'

But there was nothing to see. The slime had
vanished. Louis wondered if he was seeing things.

The noise woke half the castle. King Burt rushed in.

'What's going on here?' he asked, crossly.

'Nothing, your majesty,' said Louis. 'I just thought I saw something.'

'Are you okay, Squire Lyme?' asked King Burt. 'Did Louis scare you? I'm sorry. He's just jealous of you. The way you defeated that witch today . . . masterful.'

'About that,' started Louis. 'Hagatha isn't actually what she seems. She's not a witch at all—'

'Now stop that, Sir Louis,' said the king. 'This is all sour grapes. You are jealous of the squire. Coming here in the night to frighten him. That's very mean of you!'

'But— but—' stammered Louis.

'But nothing!' said the king. 'In fact . . . Sir Louis, you shall sleep here tonight. Squire Lyme can have your rooms. Yes. Off you go, squire!'

Everyone filed out of the room except Louis. Squire Lyme was last to leave.

'I'm so sorry about this,' he said. 'Perhaps I can cheer you up? With a gummy?'

He held out a bag of green gummies.

Louis looked into the bag . . . and took one.

'Thank you,' he said. And he popped it into his mouth.

CHAPTER 10

Don't worry! Of course, Louis didn't swallow the green gummy. He's not that daft. As soon as he was left alone, he spat the gummy out into his handkerchief and hid it inside his armour.

PHEW!   CLOSE ONE!

Then he tucked himself into the guest bed and went to sleep, feeling miserable and missing his own room. Hopefully tomorrow he could work out what was going on.

The next day he stopped by at Pearlin's laboratory.

'WHOA! What a whiff!' said Louis as he stepped inside.
'Pooh!'

Mac n Cheese still looked very unwell. The poor double-headed dragon was  wrapped up in a giant blanket and looking very unhappy.

'I'm hoping they'll feel better soon,' said Pearlin, looking worriedly at them. 'They've done some very green and stinky poos. But I think there's more to come.'

Louis gagged at the smell and cracked open a window.

'Poor Mac n Cheese. And what about Clunkalot?' asked Louis.

Pearlin pointed to a large cleaning machine.

'He's in the robot horse washer for the ninth time. I think he's getting better cos he wrote me a poem. Look.'

Pearlin showed Louis the poem that Clunkie had written after his eighth wash.

WHO SLIMED MY INNARDS?
IF I FIND THEM, THEY WILL SEE
A ROBOT'S REVENGE!

Louis handed Pearlin the gummy he had hidden in his handkerchief.

'Look at this,' he said.

'Oh thanks,' said Pearlin, and almost popped it in her mouth.

'STOP!' shouted Louis just in time. 'That's the same thing Squire Lyme gave to Mac n Cheese and Clunkie. Lyme gave me one last night. I thought you could examine it. Find out what it is.'

'Good plan,' said Pearlin. 'I'll check it out! See if it's just a gummy or . . .'

Pearlin held it up to the light. The insides of the gummy seemed to swim and slide around like a slick of green oil.

'Ugh! Looks like bogeys,' she said. 'Puts me right off eating it.'

'Thanks, Pearlin,' said Louis.

Then he headed upstairs to the Great Hall.

To his surprise, the king and the courtiers were already there, sat around the big table, and listening to Squire Lyme. The lights were low and Lyme was about to start some kind of presentation using a candle-powered projector to display pictures on the wall.

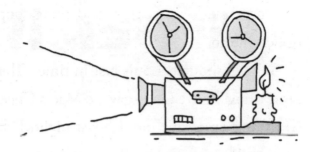

Louis hid by a pillar to watch.

CHAPTER 11

'Morning, everyone!' said Squire Lyme. 'So glad you could make it. I see Knight Sir Louis isn't here. What a slacker!'

'Oh yes,' said the king. 'A slacker. Ha ha!'

Louis noticed the king had a bag of snacks with him and was chewing on something. Gummies!

Squire Lyme turned to the king and grovelled, 'I'm especially glad that your amazing majesty King Burt the Brilliant Boss has made it. Because this morning I'd like to talk you about ogres. So, without further ado . . .'

Squire Lyme pressed a button on the remote control.

'Oh sorry! Wrong presentation!'

He pressed another button on the projector.

'Sorry again! That's tomorrow's presentation.'

He pressed the projector button again and this time it showed:

'That's the one,' he said. Then he cleared his throat and began his presentation.

'I have been a-wandering about this great country and beyond.'

'And everywhere I went I met with good people.'

'Good people who listened to my stories and ate my gummies.'

'But then I
came upon the
forest of Tumblin'
Klatterbang.
A land of wild
ogres.'

'Terrifying
ogres determined
to take over the
world and eat
everyone!'

'This plan for
world domination
starts here. They
will first try to
take over Castle
Sideways.'

'So, I propose we prepare ourselves. We must find
a way to banish all ogres from the Many Kingdoms.'

'All in favour, say aye!' said King Burt, who picked another gummy from his packet and swallowed.

Louis noticed that little plates of gummies were out all across the table in the Great Hall and everyone was helping themselves.

'No!' said Knight Sir Louis, stepping out from behind the pillar.

They all turned and stared at Louis.

'Everyone. Stop eating those gummies! And stop listening to Squire Lyme! He's up to something.'

'I'm sorry,' said Squire Lyme before turning to the king, 'but do we allow children to talk at the grown-ups' meeting?'

King Burt looked at Lyme for a moment as though working out what to say. Then suddenly he rose up looking furious and turned to Louis.

'Silence, Louis,' said the king. 'We don't need children telling us what to do. Especially ones that are slackers and cheats at playing games!'

'Why are you listening to Lyme?' said Louis. 'You don't even know him properly!'

'I said SILENCE!' said the king before burping loudly.

BURRPP!

Louis noticed that the king looked a little greener than usual. Greener and wobblier. Greener

and wobblier and . . . more see-through. No. That
didn't make sense, did it?

The other nobles joined in, berating Louis and
being all-round meanies.

Louis felt hurt by their words. He had saved the
king from all kinds of horrible things. He'd saved
him from being a giant parsnip forever. He'd
saved King Burt and all the courtiers from being
roasted by a dragon!

Louis felt tears well in the corners of his eyes. For
a moment the courtiers' bodies seemed to stretch

and squash like half-set jellies. Was that real? Or just the tears making things seem a funny shape?

'Your majesty,' said Louis. 'Are you sure you're well? Maybe you should see Pearlin?'

'I'm perfectly well,' said the king furiously. 'And I don't need advice from a child who can't even tie his own shoelaces.'

That was *really* mean, thought Louis, especially as he could tie his own shoelaces. He just didn't need to because his shoes were made of metal.

'You know, I think it's time I made some changes around here,' said King Burt, wagging his finger at Louis. 'From now on, you're demoted to knight in charge of . . . er . . . '

Squire Lyme leaned in and whispered in the king's ear.

'Yes,' said the king. 'Knight in charge of cleaning.'

'Somebody give him a bog brush,' said Squire Lyme with a high-pitched giggle and the courtiers all laughed.

'And if I refuse?' said Louis.

'Refuse me?' said the King. 'Then you will be BANISHED!'

Everyone went quiet. A hush filled the room. It was so quiet you could have heard a pin drop on a feather cushion. That's very quiet. What would Louis do?

'Banished it is!' said Louis hotly. POOH TO YOU! POOH TO YOU ALL!'

The courtiers gasped and shook their heads. Louis had defied the king! What a shocker!

Louis turned on his shiny metal heels and stomped out. But as he reached the doorway, he hid and stopped to listen.

'Well . . . you know what this means, sir,' said Lyme to the king. 'It means you need a new champion knight.'

'Oh yes!' said the king, scratching his head.

'But we don't have any other knights. What can we do?'

'Well, sir,' said Lyme. 'I am a squire, that's an apprentice knight. But if you promoted me. . . I'm sure I could give it a go.'

'What a splendid idea,' said the king.

'Yes,' said Lyme. 'I'm glad YOU thought of it.'

'Did I? Oh. Yes. Perhaps I did. I did. Yes. Definitely. Well, you'd better kneel.'

And so, Squire Lyme knelt before King Burt. King Burt didn't have a sword on him, so he used a very long carrot instead.

'Squire Lyme, I dub thee in the name of the Kingdom of Squirrel Helm. Arise as a knight, as our champion.'

Squire Lyme stood and allowed himself a thin smile that just showed his shiny white teeth. The king noticed that now Lyme was a knight he seemed taller and thinner somehow. But that couldn't be possible. Could it? Hmm.

'No more a squire,' said Lyme. 'How wonderful.'

'That's right,' said the king. 'Now you will be known as Knight Sir Lyme. Oh. Sir Lyme. Sir Lyme. That's interesting. Sounds like slime, doesn't it!'

'Yes, sir,' smiled Sir Lyme, evilly. 'What a coincidence.'

CHAPTER 12

Louis couldn't believe it. He skulked off, unable to listen to any more. He headed for Pearlin's laboratory, but he found she'd gone out. She'd left a note.

Hey Louis,

Just popped out to get some more giant-sized toilet paper for the dragon.

Back as soon as poss.

P

So he wrote her a quick note in return . . .

Hey Pearlin,

I'm off. Officially banished. When you find out what that gummy is, let me know. Send one of your 'thinking drinks' or something to find me. Good luck and be careful!

All the best

Your friend

Louis

He gave Mac n Cheese a stroke on the heads.

'Get well soon,' he said. 'And if you do another big stinky poo, consider doing it on Lyme's stupid head.'

Then Louis jumped on the back of the cleaned Clunkalot and flew out of the lab, the castle and off to . . .

. . . where?
He was so
annoyed he

didn't even know where he was going.

Clunkie could tell that Louis wasn't feeling right. So he printed him out a poem.

STUFF CASTLE SIDEWAYS!
LET'S START A NEW ADVENTURE.
YOU'RE STILL MY CHAMPION.

'Aw. Thanks Clunkie.'

And suddenly he knew where he wanted to be. More than anywhere else in the world. The place where all heroes go when there is nowhere else to go!

THE TEMPLE OF THE GODS ?   THE CAVE OF WONDERS ?   THE PLANET OF THE POSERS?

CHAPTER 13

Louis and Clunkalot flew west until they almost reached the sea. At last, they saw the home of Louis' parents, Chivalry Farm. The farm building stood in the middle of a patchwork of fields.

It looked very peaceful. But this hadn't always been the case. The farm had come under attack from all kinds of things in the past: evil witches, giant people-eating plants, sea-dragons, and a naughty company that wanted to knock down the farm and build hundreds of tiny castles all over the fields.

Louis had asked his friend Mysto (the world's greatest wizentor) to help his parents by creating a special defence system. Louis' dad Ned thought it

was a fantastic idea. Louis' mum, the Champion
Trixie, wasn't so sure.

Mysto's self-defence system was as good as he'd promised. As soon as he turned it on, it stopped anything or anyone getting near the farm.

DON'T WORRY. NO ONE IS GOING TO BE ABLE TO GET THROUGH THIS SELF-DEFENCE SYSTEM.

Unfortunately, this included the postman, the milkman and the entire local guild of knights who were wondering why Trixie wasn't at the Curry Knight Night.

Even worse, Trixie, Ned and Mysto were all trapped on the farm and unable to leave. The self-defence system was so good, it wouldn't let anything come OR go.

Before we really get into the action, let's look at a couple of pages from **Mysto's Massive Manual of All the Things I've Made.**

Here's a giant robot that Mysto made a while back.

The Damsel of Distresse had been broken up after a big fight with a potato waffle. (Long story! See *Knight Sir Louis and the Dreadful Damsel*.) But Mysto was an eco-friendly sort of dwarf, so he liked to recycle. His new self-defence system was made from the remains of the Damsel of Distresse.

FLYING DAMSEL HEAD WITH LASER TONGUE

FREE ROAMING STOMPING LEGS

ALL COATED WITH NEW SUPER TOUGH MAGIC PAINT.

And here's another of his inventions . . . Dave.

CHAPTER 14

Louis and Clunkie flew down towards Chivalry Farm. As soon as they crossed over the drystone wall of the outer fields, things got tricky. An alarm sounded and a barn near the house flipped back to reveal the head of the enormous Damsel. The head also had a henin attached – an enormous conical hat with a long veil.

Rockets fired and the head flew up and straight for Louis.

'PREPARE TO BE LASERED, TRESPASSER!' shouted the head.

'What's that doing here?' said Louis surprised.

The Damsel head starting firing! A laser bolt

AGH! slammed into Clunkie's left wing and suddenly he was spinning out of control and Louis was thrown to the ground. Luckily (or unluckily) he landed in a huge pile of manure.

Louis shouted, 'Clunkie, start digging! Go underground. Get to the farm.'

Clunkalot didn't have to be asked twice. His metal front hooves turned to shovels and he started digging as fast as he could, like a giant mole. Meanwhile the Damsel head came back to fire again. This time, Louis was ready and raised his sword.

HLOMBooSHoo!

The laser bolts flicked off Dave's blade. As the head flew past, Louis slashed out but Dave's sharp edge barely made a mark on the head.

'PATHETIC!' laughed the Damsel head. 'I'VE HAD A PAINT UPGRADE!'

Meanwhile, the
two giant stomping
legs joined the
fight, heading
for Louis'
position.

STOMP STOMP STOMP

'Oh no,' thought Louis. 'They're going to boot me off the farm. And possibly into outer space.'

But this gave him an idea. He saw the head coming back. So, he ran hard for one of the legs. He timed it just right . . . and the leg BOOTED him hard . . . and he flew through the air.

WHOOOAA! And landed on the flying head! YES! It tried to shake Louis off.

'HOW DARE YOU, TINY WORM,' shouted the head.

Louis found that by leaning to one side or the other he could drive the head around where he wanted it to go. He headed straight for the first leg and bumped into it . . . sending it crashing into the second leg. This upset the second leg and it started kicking the first one. Now, the two legs were too busy kicking each other to think about Louis. Result!

But then . . . the head tipped sharply.

'OFF YOU VILE TICK!' screamed the Damsel head.

Louis flew through the air.

WAHHHH!

And landed once more . . .

SQUELCH

. . . in a large pile of manure.

Now the head came back round to laser Louis. But he ran behind the fighting legs. The head didn't care. It wanted to zap Louis and it bowled itself into the legs, knocking them both down. The head spun out of control and hit the muddy field just in front of Louis. Louis was sent flying again and once more . . .

The legs jumped up. Now they were more annoyed with the head than with each other. So, they kicked the head back and forth between them like a football.

BOP! BOINK! BOOP! CLANG!

Oi! I SAY STOP THAT! WHOSE SIDE ARE YOU ON? Oi!

Just then a short figure ran out of Clunkie's tunnel. It was Mysto the wizentor! He ran up close to one of the legs and waved a triple-headed electro-wand at them!

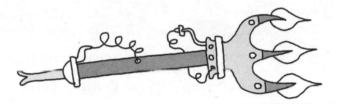

It zapped them all and at last, the legs and the head shut down.

PHEW!

Mysto looked around for his friend Louis, hoping to thank and congratulate him for saving the day.

'Louis? Louis, where are you?'

A huge pile of dung rose up in front of him and spoke.

'Mysto! Long time no see. Give us a hug!'

Mysto didn't know it was Louis covered in manure, so he did what any sensible person would do. That's right. He screamed, ran backwards and fell down Clunkie's tunnel.

WAHHHH!

MYSTO?
YOU ALRIGHT?

CHAPTER GUMMY

Let's take a quick detour back to Castle Sideways. What's going on there?

MM, I JUST LOVE THESE GUMMIES.

Oh dear. I don't like the look of that. Let's get back to Louis.

CHAPTER 15

It was the next day. Louis had slept like a baby.

YOU MEAN, HE
SPENT THE NIGHT
CRYING?

AND DID A
POO IN HIS
NAPPY?

AND NEEDED
MILK EVERY
THREE HOURS?

Okay, okay . . . Louis didn't sleep like a baby.
Louis slept like someone having a very good sleep.
(Though he did have a very strange dream about
a bowl of fruit rotting, turning into a green blob
and then oozing away down the street.)

The next day, he woke early and made breakfast for his mum and dad. Louis decided to break the news to his parents.

'I've decided to quit being a knight,' said Louis while serving up bacon and eggs.

'WHAT!?' said his parents.

'But son,' said Ned, 'you're a champion. Like your mum!'

'What's brought this on?' asked Trixie.

'I lost my job at Castle Sideways. This new guy turned up and soon everyone was laughing at me. I thought he was up to something fishy . . . but maybe I was just jealous? Maybe he was right. Maybe I don't know what I'm doing?'

'Absolute hogwash,' said Trixie. 'Look what you did yesterday against the flying head and the stomping legs.'

'But anyone could have done that,' said Louis.

'Yeah, right,' said Ned chuckling. 'Anyone. Do you think I could have done it?'

'Dad!'

'Come on! Do you? Honestly.'

'Well. No.'

'Of course not, son. I couldn't fight my way out of a paper bag. But you . . . you're something special.'

'You're special too, Dad,' said Louis. 'No one knows how to grow a parsnip like you.'

'True,' said Ned. 'When it comes to fruit and vegetables, I'm a champion. But they aren't very helpful when it comes to defeating wizards and dragons are they? Ha ha! Imagine defeating a dragon with a cucumber. Not going to happen, is it?'

'Funny you should say that,' said Louis, 'because only last month, I—'

But Trixie interrupted, 'I say that if things didn't work out with King Burt, then that's HIS problem. What you need is a new job at a new castle.'

And Trixie gave Louis a big hug to cheer him up.

CHAPTER 16

Louis went outside to find Clunkie. Clunkalot was in the large yard outside the flip-top barn. Mysto was there, working on his broken wing.

'Sorry about the defence system yesterday, Louis,' chuckled Mysto. 'Made it a wee bit too defendy. I think it was still a bit evil. When I made the original robot I was under an evil curse. I think it rubbed off.'

'How's Clunkie?' asked Louis.

'Not bad,' said Mysto. 'Clunkie's an impressive creation! That Pearlin really knows what she's doing. Anyway, I fitted him with some new wings. These have magnesium alloy feathers for an extra smooth ride.'

Clunkalot flapped his new wings experimentally. He was impressed and printed out a poem.

A FLAMINGO FLEW
FABULOUS, FLOWING, FLYING
FLAPPY BUT HAPPY

'That's nice,' said Mysto. 'Now, why don't you give them a try?'

Clunkalot jumped and flapped his new wings . . . and then they flew off on their own. They were so strong, they'd detached, leaving Clunkie grounded.

FLAP FLAP FLAP
FLAP

'Oh! Whoopsie!' said Mysto. 'Don't worry. I'll make another pair.'

'So, any other problems with Clunkie?' asked Louis.

'Aye. There was one other problem,' admitted Mysto. 'Not really one. More like eighty or ninety problems.'

'What?' said Louis, worried that Clunkie was somehow beyond repair.

'Well,' said Mysto. 'I thought I'd open Clunkie's inner compartment up to see if anything needed fixing in there. And I found these . . .'

Mysto pointed inside the barn. Louis leant over and looked inside. It was full of gnomes.

'Ohhhh yes!' said Louis. 'I completely forgot about them.'

General Gnomus approached Louis and Mysto. He looked extremely miffed.

'Forgot about us, did you?' huffed the general. 'Thought as much.'

'Sorry,' said Louis. 'I was going to bring you before the king

and have you thrown in the dungeons . . . but it slipped my mind.'

'Well, lucky your iron horse comes equipped with rations. We ate all your tins of baked beans.'

'Aye,' said Mysto, 'it was pretty smelly when I opened that door. Pooh! Lucky there were no naked flames or there might have been an explosion.'

'So, what happens now?' said General Gnomus. 'Are we to fight each other again?'

'No thanks,' said Louis. 'I'm no longer champion of Castle Sideways. And if you're looking for a new home . . . why don't you stay here with my parents? You could be their new security defence system.'

'Hmm,' said Gnomus, thinking about it. 'Only if we can have one of these fields to turn into a beautiful garden, with some ponds, and toadstools and a pretty little fountain.'

'I think Mum and Dad would like that,' said Louis.

Then he remembered he had an important question to ask the general.

'One thing, general. Why did you try to attack Castle Sideways? Was it something to do with ogres?'

'Ogres? No!' said Gnomus. 'Our town of Snoozin-By-The-Pond was overrun by great green blobs! We came north to find a new home. Your castle looked perfect for hiding from slimy monsters.'

'Interesting,' said Louis. 'Well, I hope you like it here. I'm off to find a new job.'

'I'm off too,' said Mysto. 'I'm going to do some time-travelling again.'

'Have you invented some more time shoes?' asked Louis.

'Not shoes this time,' said Mysto with a look of glee. He held up a jar of dark, speckled powder. 'I've invented time pepper!'

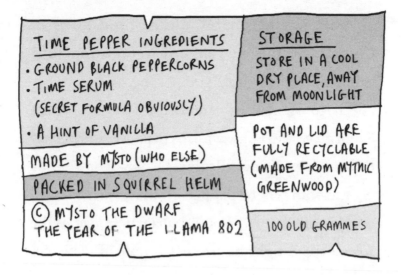

TIME PEPPER INGREDIENTS
- GROUND BLACK PEPPERCORNS
- TIME SERUM
  (SECRET FORMULA OBVIOUSLY)
- A HINT OF VANILLA

MADE BY MYSTO (WHO ELSE)

PACKED IN SQUIRREL HELM

© MYSTO THE DWARF
THE YEAR OF THE LLAMA 802

STORAGE
STORE IN A COOL
DRY PLACE, AWAY
FROM MOONLIGHT

POT AND LID ARE
FULLY RECYCLABLE
(MADE FROM MYTHIC
GREENWOOD)

100 OLD GRAMMES

INSTRUCTIONS

SIMPLY ADD A SMALL AMOUNT OF THIS TASTY
CONDIMENT TO A MEAL TO TRAVEL IN TIME.
ONE BLACK PEPPER GRAIN WILL TRANSPORT YOU
ONE WEEK BACK IN TIME. ONE WHITE PEPPER
GRAIN WILL TRANSPORT YOU ONE WEEK INTO THE
FUTURE. SIMPLY SELECT THE TYPE AND
NUMBER OF GRAINS REQUIRED AND THEN EAT.

'Well, just be careful with it,' said Louis to Mysto. 'Every time you invent time travelling thingamies, something goes wrong.'

'Of course, I'll be careful,' said Mysto. 'What could go wrong anyway? This pepper is the perfect invention. And it smells divine!'

And with that he popped off the lid and inhaled deeply. Too deeply. He snorted a whole load of the spicy pepper right up inside his nose. The pepper tickled his nose hairs (and he had a lot of nose hair).

ATCHOOOO!

Mysto vanished into the past, or the future.

WHO KNOWS WHEN?

WHO KNOWS WHO?

WHO KNOWS WHAT?

WHAT KNOWS HOW?

STOP IT!

CHAPTER 17

Louis travelled around to see if there were any castles in need of champions. But it turned out most castles and towns already had champion knights.

CASTLE ROUND THE TWIST

I'M NOW PRESIDENT
HERE, BUT I'M STILL
KNIGHT SIR DAISY TOO,
CHAMPION OF KLAPTRAP.

NO WORRIES,
GOOD
LUCK

THE TOWN OF PORTLY WISHWASH
HOME OF KNIGHT SIR MERRY-JINGLES

KNIGHT PROTECTOR
AND ALSO TOP
LOCAL COMEDIAN.

CASTLE SINGALONG

KNIGHT SIR LYLA

LA LA LA LA LA LA LA

CASTLE GIGGLES

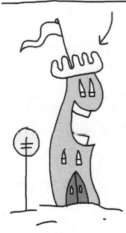

KNIGHT SIR AUDREY

HEE HEE HEE HEE HEE HEE HEE

CASTLE GOLFALOT

THWACK!

FORE!

KNIGHT SIR FINTY

It seemed hopeless. Nowhere needed a knight. But then Louis went to visit his friend Knight Sir Gary on the Isle of Tippinitdown. It was the wettest place Louis had ever been. Even wetter than the hill town of Soggy Hoo which is usually inside a rain cloud. Even wetter than the Kingdom of Turbot, which is saying something because that's underwater.

Somehow, Sir Gary always managed to look on the bright side of things, despite the terrible weather. This was just what Louis needed. Someone who could give him some hope.

'You've come to the right place, Louis!' Gary said.

'Why? Do you need another champion? You're retiring?'

'Ha! Me? No way. But I had this amazing fight with a whole bunch of pirates last week. They said they'd raided a castle on the coast near the forests of Tumblin' Klatterbang. Castle Blunder it's called. The pirates said the raid was a total breeze because the castle didn't have a champion. There was no one to defend it! I bet they would love you as their champ!'

Knight Sir Louis perked up. At last, a castle that needed a knight!

'It'll be tough to find though,' warned Gary. 'The sea route is stuffed with pirates and rocks and sea monsters. Better to go overland, through ogre country. Though they say those forests are full of dangerous plants as well as dangerous ogres . . .'

'I'll handle the ogres,' said Louis. 'And as for the plants . . . I just so happen to have a friend who's an expert in Weird Botany.'

CHAPTER 49

And so . . . hang on . . . chapter 49?

That can't be right.

We just had chapter 17!

This is no place for a chapter 49!

What are you doing here?

WELL ACTUALLY, I'M FROM THE END OF THE LAST BOOK

KNIGHT SIR LOUIS AND THE DRAGON OF DOOOOOOM!?

CHAPTER 18

You may be wondering, what was happening at Castle Sideways. What was King Burt up to? How was Sir Lyme settling in? Let's check out some of Pearlin's notes and find out.

Thoosday 10:45AM.

Just got back to the lab and found a note from Louis. I can't believe it! He's been booted out of the castle. What's King Burt doing? He must be off his rocker!

Time to do some tests on this green gummy thing!

Thoosday 11:00AM.

Got the gummy set up on my magical microscope and whoa there's something weird going on inside. Here's what I can see...

. . . like a load of tiny green faces. And not nice happy faces. This is some kind of magic I've not seen before. Is this why poor Mac n Cheese have been so ill? Better check their poops under the microscope.

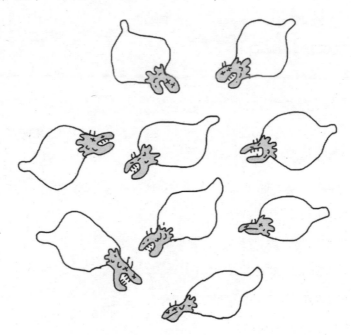

Thoosday 11:15AM.
Looks like whatever was inside the gummy didn't quite survive the dragon's stomach. Not surprised! It's hotter than the sun in

there. Oh, hang on . . . someone's bangin'
on my door. I'm gonna send off a 'thinking
drink' with my findings to Louis. Hope he
gets it!

Thoosday 12:45PM.
Just had the weirdest half hour ever. King
Burt asked me to come and see him and
that Sir Lyme. He ordered me to undo my
holding spell and let the witch Hagatha
Squint out of the dungeon! WHAAATTTT??!
Sir Lyme says she's apologised and is like
really sorry and wants to be my assistant.
WHAAAATTTT?? Then King Burt offered me
a handful of those gummies. I said like no
way, cos they are full of faces and stuff.

He told me it was an order! I lied and said I'd just eaten lunch and I'd have some at dinner time. And he said, you'd better! WHAAATTTT?

Even weirder . . . is how the king and everyone else in court is looking . . . sort of greener. Wobblier. More see-through. I don't like it.

Thoosday 1:45PM.

I'm back in the lab, but went to see that Hagatha Squint first, to see what's going on. She says she's had a think and wants to help around the castle. Says she's been an apprentice witch for ages and thinks she can learn a lot from me. Please, please, pretty please, she says. With a cherry on top. She reminds me of my nan. So, I feel like maybe she's telling the truth. And maybe I should let her out. But then I remembered my nan's in prison for handing out seeds that grow into monster plants so then I think maybe Hagatha is just where she should be. Behind bars.

Thoosday 2:15PM.

Okay. Time to decide. What are my choices? If I stay, the king is gonna make me eat one of them gummies and I'm going to have to let out Hagatha Squint. But I can't just run off and leave Mac n Cheese here. They're getting better, but slowly. If I stay, they might feed Mac n Cheese with more gummies too. Who knows what that's gonna do to them! I guess, there's one other option. I can try and flush out Mac n Cheese's guts with a special potion. Better stop writing now. I can hear someone knocking at the door again. I've bolted it. I don't have much time!

CHAPTER 19

Pearlin worked quickly. She grabbed a small cauldron, threw in some Scorchy Sauce, a slice of Fire Root, a sprinkle of Badaboom Chilli . . . and bound them together with a spell. She looked at Mac n Cheese desperately as she said:

Hubble hubble we're in trouble,
This'll make your belly bubble.
Hope it works to flush you out.
Lap it up now, down the spout!

Mac n Cheese slurped up the fiery hot potion.

Meanwhile Sir Lyme and the king's guard were hammering on the door to the lab. The king stood behind them, the greenest of all, the wobbliest of all, the most see-through of all.

'Open in the name of the king!' shouted a guard.

'Time for your gummies!' shouted Sir Lyme.

'KNOCK IT DOWN!' shouted King Burt.

They tried, but Pearlin had put a spell on it of course. They may as well have tried to knock down a cliff. But then Sir Lyme did something very odd indeed. He leaned forward and touched the door with his hand.

His hand suddenly turned into a slimy green version of itself, then oozed into the cracks of the door. Then Sir Lyme whispered some strange words – a spell – an incantation!

SSSSLLLLURRRRPPP OOOOZZEEEEYYY GGGLOOOPPPYY

And then suddenly the door to the lab exploded.

KABOOooM!

'GRAB THE WIZENTOR!' shouted Sir Lyme. The guards raced in.

Unfortunately for them, this happened at the exact same moment that Pearlin's hot sauce hit Mac n Cheese's dragon stomach. The reaction was powerful and fast . . . and very, very smelly.

Suddenly Mac n Cheese felt much better. Pearlin jumped onto their back, and they leapt out of the castle window and flew away.

'NOOOOOOO!' shouted the king.

'Yeah! It worked! Come on!' said Pearlin with glee.

'COME BACK AND HAVE YOUR GUMMIES!' shouted Sir Lyme.

But Pearlin wasn't going back. No way!

'Right, Mac n Cheese,' she said, 'let's find Louis!'

She took one last look behind her at Castle Sideways. There was Sir Lyme looking out of the window . . .

Then something very strange happened. Sir Lyme sort of . . . melted and turned bright green all over.

'PLAY TIME IS OVER!' said the slimy thing. And it lifted up its arms, pointed towards Pearlin and shouted . . .

OOOOOZZEEEEY
GGLOOOOPPPPY

And then suddenly everything went dark.

CHAPTER 20

Let us travel to a more civilised place. Hogford!

This pretty town is home to the most famous university in the Many Kingdoms. It was founded a thousand years ago by a very clever pig called Tractorina Swill.

Today, another very clever piggywig (more precisely, a boar) was living at the university. She was one of Knight Sir Louis' very best friends. She used to be called Mr Catalogue, thanks to the silly wizard that named her. But after studying strange and wonderful plants at the university, she became a teacher in Weird Botany. Her job title was reader, so now she was called Reader Catalogue.

HAHA! SOUNDS A BIT FUNNY.

RIGHT, COS IT SOUNDS LIKE "READ A CATALOGUE"

ER...YEAH, WE GET IT! YOU DON'T HAVE TO EXPLAIN IT.

Her middle name was Mildred but she still couldn't decide on a first name. This week she'd had a breakthrough and had chosen one. She'd been reading about a brave botanical explorer from *ye olde dayes*. She liked

the explorer's name so much, she decided to use it herself. The name was Henrietta.

HELLO EVERYONE, CALL ME HENRIETTA CATALOGUE

WHAT? SHE ATE A CATALOGUE?

No! IT'S HER NAME. HENRIETTA CATALOGUE.

STILL SOUNDS LIKE SHE ATE A CATALOGUE.

REMINDS ME OF MY COUSINS... IVOR LOTT AND MONA LOTT.

Knight Sir Louis rode into Hogford having made the long journey from his parent's farm. He found his friend Reader Catalogue queueing for lunch outside the popular Honkery café.

HONKERY CAFÉ

TODAY'S SPECIALS

GRUBLISH HONKERY

FOREST TD

CHOMBR LEGS

TTTTSURG's YOGURT

PURPLE YURKELB

SLUDGEGRASS SUSHI

'Catalogue, there you are!' said the knight happily.

'LOUIS! Woo! Great to see yous!' said Catalogue.

'How is life in Hogford?' Louis asked as they gave each other a big hug.

'All righty, I suppose,' said Catalogue. 'Bit borings if I'm honest.'

'Do you fancy going on an adventure to a dangerous forest full of ogres? Tumblin' Klatterbang to be precise,' Louis asked.

Catalogue looked excited. 'Do I?! For sure! That forest ain't well explored. Maybe I can finds some new plants and calls them after me and you, like Prunus catalogi or Quercus knightus.'

'Great! Because I need help getting to a castle down there. Castle Blunder!'

'Sounds like a disaster waiting to go boom!' said Reader Catalogue. 'You sure you want to goes?'

As they were waiting for their lunch, Louis told his friend about everything that had happened.

'So now I need a new castle and king to champion. Castle Blunder is a silly name though – perhaps I can persuade them to change the name to Castle Thunder or Castle Wonder.'

By now, Louis and Catalogue were almost at the front of the queue.

'What kind of food do they serve here?' asked Louis.

'Ogrish nosh,' said Catalogue.

Louis peered in. At the counter were a dwarf, a human and an ogre taking orders. Behind them he saw into the open kitchen where three huge ogres were busy cooking all sorts of dishes.

'Don't think I've ever had ogre food before,' he said. 'Funny. Because I recently met someone who said ogres were really bad news. That they were planning an invasion.'

'What a load of cobblers,' said Catalogue. 'Let me ask my friend.'

They reached the counter and Catalogue spoke to the ogre sitting behind the till.

'Dollop! You planning a big old invasion?' chuckled Catalogue.

'Hey Catalogue!' said Dollop with a genuine smile. 'Invade what? Maybe a cosy cave for a big century snooze. Haha!'

Louis smiled. Dollop seemed very friendly. Lyme's warnings about an ogre invasion seemed even more ridiculous than before.

'So, what's it to be?' asked Dollop, indicating the menu.

Louis had the Purple Yurkelb and Catalogue went for a double portion of Sludgegrass Sushi. Mm! Delicious.

Now seems a good moment to take a closer look at ogres. What are they exactly? Luckily, we're in Hogford and not far from the Department of Ograpology. Here's their fun factsheet for visitors.

UNIVERSITY OF HOGFORD
DEPARTMENT OF OGRAPOLOGY

Welcome. And thank you for visiting us.
Here in the D.O.O. we study all things ogrish.

Some of us here are ogres. Some of us are not.
Everyone is welcome to study.
All you need is an interest in ogres.

Some fun facts about ogres.

Ogres grow to be
giant-sized.

Ogres have stone skeletons. Granite!

Ogres do not sleep every night. In fact, they stay awake for years at a time, then find a nice cave and sleep for decades or even centuries!

Despite what you may have heard, ogres do not turn to stone in sunlight. In fact, sunlight makes their stone skeletons healthier and harder.

Ogres are nature lovers and protect their forests from invaders without mercy! Those ogres that have come to live in cities always make excellent gardeners. Some say they are even better than gnomes* at gardening.

(*Gnomes disagree, of course.)

CHAPTER 21

The next day, Catalogue and Louis climbed aboard Clunkalot, ready to ride off on their adventure south. Just before they left, Dollop came to find them.

'Wait a moment,' said the ogre. 'I've got a wotsit for you.'

Dollop lifted up a paper bag stuffed with something blue and a bit whiffy.

'Ooo! Why is you giving us raw sludgegrass?' said Catalogue.

'It's a present for my cuz,' said Dollop. 'If you're going to Tumblin' Klatterbang look out for my cousin Wurt. He loves sludgegrass but it don't grow in the forests down there.'

'We'll do our best to find him,' said Louis and he stored the bag inside Clunkie's metal belly.

'Make sure you two don't eat it though,' said Dollop. 'The raw stuff is only for stoney creatures like ogres. If you ate it, your lickle tongues would dissolve.'

And he chuckled, before looking stern. 'Seriously, don't eat it.'

'Thanks for the warning!' said Louis.

'See yous later,' said Catalogue.

And off they rode.

Which was a shame, because half an hour later, Pearlin's 'thinking drink' flew into Hogford looking for Louis. It had just missed him. It flew on . . . hoping to catch up with him.

I FLY! LIKE A DRAGON! IF DRAGONS WERE SHAPED LIKE BOTTLES.

CHAPTER 22

The last thing Pearlin remembered was making a daring escape on the back of her dragon, Mac n Cheese. So it was rather surprising to wake up in a dungeon. She heard something clattering and banging and turned to see Mac n Cheese jumping around in the cell beside hers.

'Oi, Mac n Cheese! What happened?'

Mac n Cheese hadn't really got the hang of language yet, but Mac managed to say, 'Slobber.' And Cheese managed to say, 'Magic.'

'Slobber magic?' said Pearlin. 'What does that mean?'

Someone outside the cell spoke. 'It means, me duck, you were defeated by a magic far greater than yours.'

It was Hagatha Squint.

'How did you get out?' said Pearlin. 'I left a strong holding spell on your cell!'

'Someone with better magic than yours let me out,' said Hagatha.

Pearlin thought about all the suspicious goings-on in the castle. They had all started with Lyme's arrival.

'You and that Lyme been working together the whole time, right?' guessed Pearlin. 'When you flew in on that tree and he biffed you with a baguette . . . that was all planned weren't it? You and him?'

'Oh! Well done for working that out . . . FAR TOO LATE! HA HA!' gloated Hagatha.

'So, this better magic . . . it's slobber magic, is it?'

'Oh, you should have seen it!' said Hagatha with glee. 'I peeked out of my little cell window. There you was, about to fly away forever, when my master raised his hand . . . and SPLAT . . . covered you with slime! IT WERE GLORIOUS! And very icky.'

Pearlin thought back and remembered seeing Lyme transform into a giant green blob.

'So not slobber magic . . . but SLIME magic. Whatever that is.'

'Slime magic is the greatest of all magics!' barked Hagatha.

'You sure? Cos we had a really bad wizard here before and he said potato magic was the best.'

'Potatoes! Well. . . yes. That is a powerful magic. But NOTHING compared to slime! You'll find there's no way through these bars, protected as they are, by my master's slime magic. Unless . . .'

'Unless what?' asked Pearlin.

Hagatha held out her hand and opened it. Sitting on her palm was a green gummy.

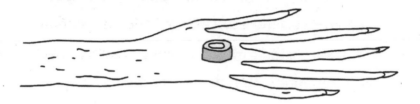

'No way!' said Pearlin.

'It's all there is to eat. I'll just leave it here.'

And she placed it just outside the bars.

Pearlin thought there was no way she was going to eat that snotty gummy, even if it was the last thing on the planet. Her mind was already whirring and trying to find a way out of this mess.

She looked at Hagatha with curiosity. 'So,

what's in it for you?' Pearlin asked. 'Why are you doing all this?'

'Because I'm a slime magic apprentice! And one day the master will turn me into a slime sorcerer just like him.'

'And that's a good thing, is it?' said Pearlin doubtfully.

'Of course it is!' barked Hagatha. 'Because slime sorcerers live FOREVER!'

'I get it,' said Pearlin. 'So, the upside is you get to be immortal. But the downside is you spend eternity being a giant blob of green snot?'

'You're just jealous that you're not his apprentice!' the witch said.

'How long have you been his apprentice, exactly?' asked Pearlin.

'Er . . . not long,' said Hagatha defensively. 'Only about sixty years.'

'SIXTY YEARS!' said Pearlin. 'Are you sure he's going to make you a slime wotsit? Sounds like he's stringing you along!'

Hagatha turned bright red with anger. 'That's enough!' she said. 'Just eat up your gummy!' And she strode out of the dungeon.

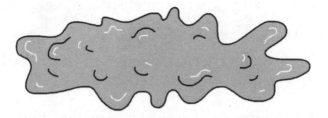

Pearlin tried a few spells to break out of the cell, but the slime magic was indeed powerful. It kept the door and the bars stuck shut.

Just then she felt her tummy rumble. She was feeling hungry.

She looked at the gummy.

There was no way she was going to eat that.

Her tummy rumbled some more.

Somehow the gummy looked more appealing than before. A bit . . . yummy.

It was *something* to eat after all.

She looked across at Mac n Cheese with dismay.

'Oh M.C. what we gonna do?'

CHAPTER 23

Louis and Catalogue were sitting astride Clunkalot as he clattered down the road south through Squirrel Helm. They took the coastal path until ahead they saw the borderland where Squirrel Helm ended and where the forest of Tumblin' Klatterbang began. And what a forest it was!

Everything was giant . . . the daisies growing at the edge of the forest were the size of sunflowers. The trees were as tall as hills. (Louis hoped there weren't any wasps. He didn't like normal ones, never mind wasps the size of flying elephants.)

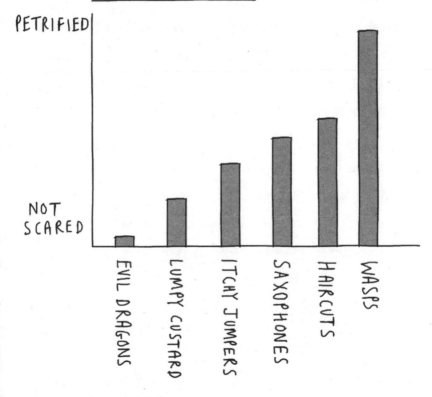

LOUIS' FEAR INDEX

They stood just outside the forest and peered between the tree trunks. Even though it was bright sunshine where they stood, it was as dark as midnight inside the forest.

'I really wish you could still fly,' said Louis to Clunkie. 'Shame those new wings flew off on their own! We could have just flown over.'

Louis, Clunkie and Reader Catalogue walked closer and stepped out of Squirrel Helm and into the forest of Tumblin' Klatterbang, under the tall trees and into the darkness.

As Clunkie stepped into the woods, he felt something stick to his foot – a piece of paper. He wiggled his leg and it fell off into the mud. If he'd stopped to read it, he would have seen it was a bulletin from the nearby town of Nervous Klench. Here's what it said:

NERVOUS KLENCH
WEEKLY BULLETIN
First Fryday of The
Month of Spider Webs

Prepared by Baron Shivering

Dear friends,

This week has been very busy in our lovely little town of Nervous Klench. Here are the highlights!

Richard Gargles won first prize in the eyebrow growing contest.

Well done, Richard! Just imagine what you can achieve next year!

Bonnie Smashington has temporarily taken over the tea shop from her aunt, Dolly Tripover.

Get well soon, Dolly. And try to be more careful this time, Bonnie!

I've also had lots of you concerned about the

slime monsters who have taken over the entire town south of the river.

It seems that there was only one invader originally . . . and that it transformed their neighbours (our fellow townsfolk) into slime monsters. Indeed, one of them is my younger brother Percy.

By way of apology, the slime monsters will be handing out some treats at the Market Hall on Friday.

The slime monsters' invitation promises that 'everyone can enjoy our free gummies. Get there early and eat as many as you can!' Join us there at 6pm!

CHAPTER 24

Back to the forest of Tumblin' Klatterbang! Let's have a look inside! Let's tune into the eyeballs of Clunkalot and see what he sees.

Wow! That is very dark indeed. Lucky that Clunkie has a night-light function. Did you know that his whole body can glow softly? Let's turn that on and see what we can see.

Oh dear. I'm starting to wish we hadn't tried that. This is all starting to remind me of chapter 1.

CHAPTER 25

Louis looked up at the trio of ogres around him. They didn't look like the smiling, friendly chefs from Honkery Café. Louis felt that if there was a café here, and it had a menu board, it might say something like:

> ≡ TODAY'S SPECIALS ≡
>
> • ROASTED KNIGHT
>   COOKED IN HIS OWN SHELL
>
> • FRESH CATALOGUE
>   SAUSAGES
>
> • CLUNKALOT AND
>   CUSTARD

His first instinct was to unleash his sword Dave and defend himself. But sometimes pulling out a sword and pointing it in people's faces can give the wrong impression. It can make you seem unfriendly. If there's ever a good time to seem friendly, it's when you find yourself surrounded by enormous bone-crushing ogres.

'Hi there!' said Louis, trying to sound casual. 'How's it . . . ogring?'

The ogres exchanged suspicious looks.

'Is he made of slime?' asked one to another.

'We could squeeze him and see if he oozes,' suggested another.

'I don't like him,' said the third. 'For a start he's dressed up his pet piggywig in clothes. That's not right!'

'Oi! I be no one's pet,' said Catalogue, crossly.

This made the ogres jump with surprise.

'HEY! A TALKING PIGGYWIG!'

'Some kind of dark magic!'

Louis knew they needed to make these ogres feel at ease and fast, so Louis, Clunkie and Catalogue introduced themselves. The ogres did the same. Their names were Moss, Petunia and Acorn. They were fascinated by Catalogue, but also a bit wary.

'I'm not an evil'un,' Catalogue said, 'and I'm no pig neither, I'm a boar! And, yes, I do haves a bigger brain than's normal. For a start, I knows bits of ogrish language. *Frgun jiml woob humb flipple yurrrr'n'go. Skark fooloo bd akul r'zo.*'

The ogres looked at each other in wonder.

Louis leaned over and whispered, 'Wow! Impressive. What did you say?'

Catalogue said, 'I'm hoping wot I said is *we come in peace* and *we're just passing through on the way to a castle*.' It seemed she was right.

'Castle?' said Moss the ogre. 'What castle?'

'Castle Blunder,' said Louis. 'Do you know it?'

'Why do you wanna go there?' asked Moss. 'There's no one there.'

'Yeah,' said Petunia. 'And it's cursed.'

'Right,' said Acorn. 'Plus, it smells of old fishes.'

Louis sighed. Being champion of an empty castle in a cursed land that smelled of fish didn't sound much fun to him.

The ogres talked amongst themselves again.

'A boar what is clever and what can talk ogrish. Something's going on,' said Moss.

'Probably a trick. We should crush 'em,' said Petunia.

Just then, Catalogue remembered the gift from Dollop. 'Oo! Hey! We got something for a chum of yours. It's tasty sludgegrass for someone wot is called . . . er . . . Worm? No . . . er . . . Wart?'

'Do you know Wurt?' said Moss.

'That little nobody!' said Petunia. 'Why does he get sludgegrass and we don't?'

The ogres seemed very confused about what to do.

'I can't work this out!' Acorn said worriedly. 'Is these visitors good'uns or bad'uns!'

'I dunno. I say let's just squeeze 'em,' suggested Petunia.

'But maybe they could help us,' said Acorn.

'I'm sure we can help,' interrupted Louis, determined to get on their side. 'I'm a knight, you see. Helping people is basically my job. What seems to be the problem?'

The ogres looked at each other.

'Blobs,' said Moss.

'Green blobs,' said Petunia.

'Wobbly see-through green blobs,' said Acorn.

Louis shivered. This was all sounding a little bit too familiar.

He asked, 'I don't suppose you know a man called Lyme?'

CHAPTER 26

A very short while later, Louis was wishing he hadn't asked that question. Because Louis, Catalogue and Clunkalot were now tied up inside a huge leather sack and slung over Moss' shoulder.

'What we gonna do nows?' asked Catalogue as they bumped up and down.

'Escape,' said Louis. 'I just need to grab Dave and cut our way out. The only problem is I'm squeezed in here so tight I can't move a muscle.'

'Maybe Clunkie can zap us out with his fizzling laser eyes,' suggested Catalogue.

Clunkie printed out a haiku for them . . .

WHEN FIRING LASERS
BE CAREFUL NOT TO ZAP-ZAP
AT YOUR TWO BEST FRIENDS

But it was so cramped no one could reach it, never mind read it.

Before they had a chance to come up with another plan, the sack was opened. Louis, Clunkalot and Catalogue tumbled out into a huge wooden cage.

They looked around. They were still in the forest, but there was a huge stone hill in front of them.

'Smuh! Ik b'lnf wergulbun?' said Catalogue in ogre language. (That's 'Eh! What's going on?' to you and me.)

'You is confusing us,' said Acorn.

'You seem like friends, speaking ogrish and saying you'll help!' said Moss.

'But you also seems like foes, saying you want to go to Castle Blunder and that you know that nasty slimy Lyme fella,' said Petunia. 'He was the one nosing around the forest and surrounding towns. And afterwards, everything went green and blobby.'

'So we've brought you here to be judged!' said Moss.

'Judged by who?' asked Louis.

'By the Eldogre,' said Acorn, and he pointed at the stony hill.

Louis looked carefully at the hill. There was something strange about the shape of it. He tipped his head on one side to get a different look. And then he saw it. The hill wasn't a hill at all, but an absolutely enormous sleeping ogre.

'I'm afraid we're all doomed,' said someone with a quiet and gentle voice.

Louis, Clunkalot and Catalogue turned. In the cage, a teeny tiny ogre was sitting beside them with a book under one arm.

'Hello, I'm Wurt.'

'Ooo, hello Wurt!' said Catalogue. 'Got some sludgegrass for you!'

CHAPTER 27

CHAPTER 28

Back in Castle Sideways, things were even stranger than before. King Burt was sitting on his throne in the Great Hall. He was now extremely green, extremely wobbly and extremely see-through. He was having trouble concentrating.

'I do like Sir Lyme. . . but I . . . er . . . what was I saying? Er . . .'

Sir Lyme entered the room with Hagatha Squint at his side. They came up close to the King.

'Yes, his majesty is about ready! Lovely.'

'Ready?' babbled the king. 'For . . . er . . . what?'

'To be de-slimed?' Hagatha asked Sir Lyme.

'Exactly,' said Lyme. 'Well done, apprentice!'
Hagatha smiled adoringly at him.

'De . . . what?' said the king, confused.

'Now watch . . .' said Lyme to Hagatha. 'Watch
what happens when you de-slime just one
slime-drone!'

'Who are you . . . er . . . calling a slime . . .
wotsit?' said the king dreamily.

'Slime-drone,' corrected Lyme with an evil
chuckle.

'Yeah, shut up, slime-drone,' added Hagatha.

Lyme continued. 'So, apprentice. As you know,

the gummies make people's bodies produce lots and lots of lovely slime. Once they are at this stage . . .' Sir Lyme poked King Burt and the king wibbled and wobbled like a huge jelly, '. . . they are ready to be de-slimed! Like this . . .'

Sir Lyme pointed a finger at the king. His finger became long and green and slimy. When it touched the king, there was a disgusting slurping sound.

CLLLLOₒOᵒ OₒOSSSS WHUMP

The slime was sucked up into Sir Lyme's body. Hagatha watched in wonder as he grew in size until he was twice as big as before!

'Now, I am twice the slime sorcerer I was before,' said Lyme with glee. 'And the king is ready to start the process all over again.'

Hagatha looked back at King Burt. For the first time in days, he looked like a proper person again.

'Goodness, what happened to me,' said the king, his thoughts suddenly as clear as day again.

(Well, as clear as they usually were anyway.) He looked up at Lyme.

'Knight Sir Lyme! What's going on? What are you up to? And why are you twelve feet tall?'

'I'll explain everything,' said Lyme silkily, 'but first, why don't you have some gummies!'

'I'm not eating any more of your . . . oh. . . gummies. Mmm! Yes please!'

And silly King Burt popped one in his mouth and started chewing. The whole process was about to start again.

'Soon, he'll be a slime-drone once more,' chuckled Lyme.

He headed out with Hagatha. 'Now, let us find the other courtiers. There's more slime to collect!'

Hagatha followed and gathered the courage to ask, 'So master, when will you make me into a slime sorcerer? Will it be soon?'

'Oh yes!' reassured Lyme. 'Very soon. So soon. Soon soon soon.'

'Oh good,' said Hagatha and she stopped and watched him turn a corner. Then she said to herself, frustrated, 'But when exactly is *soon*?'

CHAPTER 29

Pearlin was still down in the dungeon. She had tried several different spells for unlocking the dungeon door, but none had worked. Whatever this slime magic was, it was powerful!

She was still hungry. But she had resisted eating the gummy. She knew that would be a very bad idea. But being hungry wasn't helpful. It made it harder to think up a really good plan. She looked over at Mac n Cheese in the next cell.

'If only we could squeeze between the bars, eh?' said Pearlin.

'Squeeze,' said Mac.

'Squeeze,' said Cheese.

'Yeah, squeeze,' said Pearlin.

And then there it was. An idea.

She picked up the gummy and squeezed it. She remembered the horrible little faces inside the gummy. She remembered that there weren't many after Mac n Cheese had eaten one and pooped it out.

'Come here, Mac n Cheese,' she said and laid the gummy down on the floor near them. 'Give that a roasting, will ya?'

Mac n Cheese looked at the tiny gummy, shrugged and then let out a little stream of blue fire.

The gummy bubbled and started to melt.

'Stop!' ordered Pearlin. 'That's enough.'

She waited for it to cool, and then picked it up and swallowed it.

Mac n Cheese looked alarmed and shook their heads.

'No no no!' they said.

'It might not work,' said Pearlin, 'but I'm hoping you've knocked out most of the bad magic.'

She walked up to the bars to the dungeon cell and pushed herself between two of the bars.

'But I'm hoping there's just enough slime magic left to make me . . . squeeeeeezable'

And sure enough, Pearlin squeezed through the bars and out the other side.

'Nice one!' she said. 'I'll be back to let you out as soon as, Mac n Cheese. But first I gotta get back to my lab!'

CHAPTER 30

Usually the word 'ogre' conjures up images of:

GINORMOUS GIANTS!

TITANIC TEETH!

MASSIVE MEATY FEET!

FEROCIOUS FIGHTING FISTS!

CLONKING CLUBS!

But with Wurt, it was more like . . .

HUGELY HELPFUL!

UNEXPECTEDLY UNDERSIZED!

Wurt was quite small because he was still young for an ogre. He was only fifty-one. Little more than a boy. Aw!

In the cage, Catalogue opened up Clunkalot and handed over the sludgegrass from Wurt's cousin in Hogford.

'Oh! Thank you,' said Wurt politely. 'That's nice of Dollop. Shame I don't really like it.'

'So, what's going on here?' Louis asked.

'We are waiting to be judged by the great Eldogre,' explained Wurt.

THE ELDOGRE FACTSHEET!

NAME: Eldogre (as in old ogre)

AGE: Really massively old

FAVOURITE COLOURS: Sky-blue and cloudy-white

FAVOURITE ANIMAL: Forest Mammoth

JOB: Judge! The Eldogre listens and judges. She is fair-minded.

'And what did you do wrong?' asked Louis.

'Oh, I wrote a book,' Wurt said, holding it up.

'Wow! Sounds brilliant!' said Louis.

'Thanks,' said Wurt. 'Yeah. I always loved reading, and always wanted to be a knight, but the other ogres didn't like it. Said it wasn't right. But they weren't sure, so they said I'd have to come and be judged by the Eldogre.'

'What did this Eldogre be saying?' asked Catalogue.

'Nothing, of course,' said Wurt. 'She's asleep. We're supposed to wait here until she wakes up.'

'How long will that be?' Louis asked.

'Well, they say last time she woke up was two hundred years ago,' said Wurt, 'so could be tomorrow . . . could be in a thousand years.'

'And we're not allowed to go until then?' Louis said.

'Right,' said Wurt. 'I've tried to wake her up . . . but nothing's worked.'

The three bigger ogres, Moss, Petunia and Acorn rattled the wooden cage.

'Course it's not worked,' said Moss. 'You is just a puny ogre. Who cares what you thinks?'

'Yeah!' said Petunia. 'Too young to know any better.'

'Though his book was good,' said Acorn, thoughtfully.

Moss and Petunia looked at him accusingly.

'Er . . . not that I read it,' lied Acorn. 'Or can read. Or have a library of my own books at home. Er . . . I think I'll just stop talking.'

'Yeah, shut up, Acorn!' said Moss.

The three ogres continued to argue.

Wurt sulked. 'I suppose they're right. I am the youngest, smallest and therefore, probably the most stupid ogre that ever there was.'

This all reminded Louis of Squire Lyme and all the nasty things he'd said to Louis. And it made him angry. Louis wasn't standing for this.

'Now listen here, Wurt. Just because we're young doesn't mean we're useless. Let me tell you, I've met plenty of grown-ups who are total nincompoops!'

TOP TEN GROWN-UP NINCOMPOOPS!

JINGO BINGO
THE SWALLOWER OF EXTRA LONG SWORDS

FELICITY TUCKSHOP
CREATOR OF THE CHOCOLATE OVEN GLOVE

WINKLE VAN CRINKLE
INVENTOR OF METAL BISCUITS

MELLY BONCHERS
BAKER OF HAIR PIES

TERENCE TITTLE-TATTLE
LIAR EXTRAORDINAIRE

NERVOUS JIM GROT
SABRE-TOOTHED-RABBIT TAMER

SPLENDID DAN
BANJO BREAKER

HARRIET FLUFFKIN
BUILDER OF CHEESE HOUSES

GINA LIMPET
WORLD RECORD FOR MOST
AMOUNT OF NOSE PICKING

MAVIS JAWBONE-BUCKET
LEADER OF THE
EVERYONE-MUST-WEAR A
MASSIVE POWDERED-WIG
PARTY

'It seems to me there's only one way out of here,' said Louis. 'We must wake the Eldogre!'

CHAPTER 31

'No-one's ever woken up the Eldogre,' said Acorn.

'She just wakes up when she's ready,' said Petunia.

'It's true. I tried shouting, stamping, stomping, singing, screaming,' said Wurt. 'But she didn't seem to hear.'

Louis leafed through Wurt's book. If he was going to be stuck in a cage for decades, at least he'd have a good book to read. But then, a thought struck him.

'You know, your book about Knight Sir David has given me an idea,' said Louis and he held up his sword. 'My sword's called Dave and he's magical. He can slice through almost anything.

He can reflect dragon fire. He can repel evil spells. But there's one other power he has . . .'

'Oh, don't be saying you're gonna let him sings,' said Catalogue worriedly.

'That's right,' said Louis. 'Dave loves to sing.'

'And it sounds so nasty, you thinks your trotters is gonna fall off and run away by themselves,' explained Catalogue to Wurt.

'But maybe . . .' said Wurt cottoning on, 'it could wake up the Eldogre?'

'Right!' said Louis and he turned to Clunkalot. 'You know what to do, Clunkie.'

Clunkie started to spin his tail around and around.

Soon, the air was whipping across the sharp edge of Dave's blade. And he started to sing . . .

It sounded awful. Louis, Catalogue, Wurt and Clunkie all covered their ears. Moss, Petunia and Acorn were also bent double, trying to bury their heads deep in the soil. In fact, the singing was so bad that even the trees nearby tried to cover their ears with their hands and, well, that's impossible because . . . they don't have ears and hands.

But there is one group of animals that absolutely love Dave's singing.

Walruses.

We all know that walruses like:

THE SEA?   A FISH SUPPER?   VERY LARGE TOOTHBRUSHES?

Yes to all of those. But they also like Dave's singing.

Why?

No idea!

It wasn't long before walruses were flopping and squirming their way through the forest, which is not their natural habitat at all. Think about it. When was the last time you saw a walrus in a forest? But the sound of Dave's singing was irresistible to them.

'I think Dave's sounding even sharper than usual!' said one in walrus language.

'A first-class concert! Even better than that one underwater!' said another who'd been lucky enough to hear Dave slicing water in the deep sea.

'This one's going on longer than normal too,' said a third, very pleased that Dave's song was going on and on and on.

Louis and his chums weren't so happy about that. But then Louis saw the huge hill start to move very slightly.

Sure enough, the vile hideous sound of Dave's singing was disturbing the long, dreamy sleep of the massive Eldogre.

Louis lowered Dave and Clunkie stopped spinning his tail. The dreadful concert was over and everyone was happy.

(Except for the walruses of course.)

'I think it's working!' said Louis pointing at the unfolding hill, and they all looked.

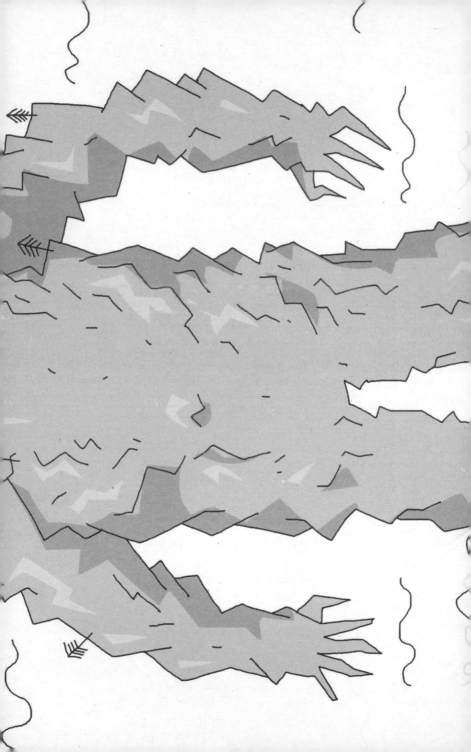

'Wowsies, not something you sees every day,' said Catalogue. 'A hill standing up and yawning.'

'Yaaaaawwwwwwnnnnn!' said the Eldogre in a voice as loud as thunder, but as smooth as a flowing river. **'Oh dear. I think I've overslept again. What time is it?'**

'The Year of Our Llama 802,' replied Louis.

'Goodness me,' said the Eldogre. **'I've been asleep for decades. Centuries. That explains why I'm so hungry and . . . oh dear . . . really need a wee-wee.'**

CHAPTER 32

A short time later the Eldogre was feeling much better. She'd gone behind a few trees and answered the call of nature. But she was still hungry. So she ate up all the bushes and trees and mushrooms that had become stuck to her over the years.

Catalogue waved up at her. 'Eh! Uh! 'Scuse me your massiveness, but are you fancying a portion of sludgegrass? It's not big and all, but it is raw and real tasty!'

The Eldogre's eyes almost popped out with excitement. (Metaphorically speaking, you know. Not actually. If her huge diamond eyes had really popped out, they would have squashed Louis, Catalogue and everyone else.)

The Eldogre was delighted with the gift of raw sludgegrass and she swallowed it down in one gulp.

'Ooooooooo, that makes waking up totally worth it,' said the Eldogre. **'Now, what's going on here? Why have you woken me up?'**

Petunia stood forward and explained. 'Oh! Great Eldogre! We don't know if this lot are good'uns or bad'uns. We need your wis . . . um . . . wis . . . er . . .'

'Wisdom?'

'Yeah, that's it!'

'Very well! Who's first?'

'Er . . . I think that's me, Wurt,' said Wurt bravely and he stepped forward.

'Wurt? Good name. What a young thing you are!' said the Eldogre, not unkindly. **'Then, let the trial of Wurt begin!'**

And so . . .

Yea! Louis and his friends did stand inside their wooden cage before the mighty Eldogre.

Yea! They did wait for judgement!

Yea! They did look upon the enormous ogre in wonder and fear and hope.

And then did Catalogue turn to Louis and say, 'If you'd been telling me this morning that I'd be a prisoner in a weird old forest, going to the trial of a tiny ogre with three other big ogres and one totally enormo-giganto-massive ogre wots been asleep for centuries, I'd have said . . . sounds like a chunky day of fun.'

Louis smiled at his friend. 'I agree. This is exactly why I like being a knight.'

'So why have you been sent here? Have you been naughty, Wurt?' asked the Eldogre.

'He wrote a book!' shouted Moss the ogre. 'We're not sure that's very ogrish!'

'It's a big book too, with pictures and words and everything,' shouted Petunia.

'I see!' said the Eldogre. **'So you wrote a book.**

Something no ogre in this forest has done for many a long year. What shall we do with you, Wurt?'

Louis decided to lend a helping hand. He stepped up beside Wurt, put an arm around his shoulder, and looked up at the Eldogre

'I've got an idea,' he shouted up. 'Why don't we let Wurt read us a bit?'

'Hmmmmmmmmmmm! Interesting. Yes. I'll allow it.'

'Is that a good idea?' wondered Moss aloud.

'Oh yes! I'd love to hear it again,' said Acorn, before quickly saying, 'er . . . for the first time.'

So Wurt opened his book and read, 'Knight Sir David the 523rd.'

Now, I know you'd like to read that book too. But we can't fit a whole other book inside this book, otherwise it would get really thick. So let's just check out the back cover for details.

KNIGHT SIR DAVID THE 523RD
BY WURT AND INSPIRED BY C.TAYLOR

SIR DAVID THE OGRE OF AQUASHELL PALACE IS HOPING FOR A HOLIDAY IN GIANT SHELL CAVE! BUT THEN SOMEBODY POURS SHRINKING POTION ONTO HIS FAVOURITE MEAL OF BOILED DRAGONFLIES.

CAN SIR DAVID WORK OUT WHO THE VILLAIN IS, BEFORE THEY SHRINK EVERYONE IN THE KINGDOM? IT'S TIME TO CLIMB ABOARD SIR DAVID'S STEED THE GIGANTIC SPARROW AND VISIT HIS BEST FRIEND, THE SCIENTIST DR CLEVER CLOGGS!

CHAPTER 33

Pearlin was sneaking around her own laboratory back at Castle Sideways. She found her books of magic and searched through them for anything on slime magic. Nothing!

What should she do? she wondered.

She couldn't hang around here too long. The courtiers would find her and make her eat a proper gummy. And she'd seen some of them sliding along the corridors. The slime magic had really taken effect.

Pearlin decided to try escaping again. But this time, she'd do it more quietly without causing a fuss. And she'd go to a place where maybe, just maybe, there were books about slime magic.

As quickly as she could, she whipped up a very special potion.

As night fell, she sneaked back downstairs to the dungeon. She squeezed herself through the bars into Mac n Cheese's cell and climbed on board their back.

'Get ready for some gliding Mac n Cheese, yeah? Nothing flashy. Nice and quiet. And no fire!'

Mac n Cheese both grinned and turned to face the dungeon wall.

Pearlin hurled the potion she'd made at the wall.

The wall exploded.

Very very quietly.

BOOM!

Pearlin and Mac n Cheese flew out and away from Castle Sideways. Luckily for them it was a moonless and cloudy night, so it was too dark for anyone to see them go. But it also meant that Pearlin failed to notice the crowds of people walking silently through the night towards the castle – crowds of green and wobbly slightly see-through people . . .

CHAPTER 34

In the forest of Tumblin' Klatterbang, Wurt finished reading his book and closed it. Louis and Catalogue clapped. Clunkalot stamped his feet in appreciation.

'Now that's what I call a right boom-boom-bash of a story,' said Catalogue.

'I really loved the bit where the knight fought a giant crumpet. Something like that happened to me once,' said Louis.

Even the ogres seemed impressed by the story.

WAS ACTUALLY PRETTY FUN.

I LIKE THE OGRE BEING THE HERO.

TOLD YOU IT WAS GOOD.

Now all eyes turned to the Eldogre. What did she think? After all, it was her judgement that really counted.

The Eldogre looked very thoughtful. Then after a moment she leaned down until her huge head was close to Wurt's.

'Wurt is a good name,' said the Eldogre. **'I have a son called Wurt. He's always been a very good boy.'**

'Yes, I know,' said Wurt anxiously. 'He's my great granddad. I'm Wurt the Fourth, you see.'

'So, we're family?' said the Eldogre with a smile before adding, **'That's good. But it doesn't mean I'm going to do you any favours!'**

Louis was worried. Was the Eldogre going to punish Wurt? Did no one old think young people were worthwhile?

'Because even if we weren't family, I would still say . . . that is the best story I've ever heard! You must give me a copy, so that I can read it again. Though you'll need to make me a much larger book of course!'

Everyone sighed with relief.

Louis smiled. The Eldogre clearly thought a 'young'un' like Wurt *was* worth listening to. Not like Lyme or King Burt.

Louis stepped forward bravely. 'I suppose that means it's our turn to be judged,' he said.

'And what is your name, young knight? I don't think we are related, are we?'

I DON'T THINK SO, SADLY. MY NAME
IS KNIGHT SIR LOUIS, AND THIS IS
MY FRIEND CATALOGUE AND MY
TRUSTY STEED CLUNKALOT.

'**Knight Sir Louis?**' said the Eldogre. '**Now, that is interesting. I have heard your name before!**'

This confused everyone, because Louis was only twelve and the Eldogre had been asleep for two hundred years. Before anyone had time to ask what she meant, the Eldogre swept her palms together, breaking the wooden cage and gathering up everyone – Louis, Catalogue, Clunkie, Wurt and the three ogres too.

'**Come on!**' she said. '**There's someone waiting to meet you!**'

And the Eldogre strode off westwards through the great wood.

'Where's we going?' asked Catalogue.

CHAPTER 35

CHAPTER 36

Pearlin and Mac n Cheese had escaped Castle Sideways. They'd flown all night just in case someone came after them. Pearlin didn't want to get caught a second time!

The next morning, they flew into Hogford where Catalogue usually lived. Hogford was known for its excellent university and library.

Here's the library. It's shaped like a brain. Yes, I know it's a bit weird.

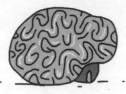

But that wasn't the weirdest thing today. Because Pearlin looked down and saw that the people of Hogford weren't their usual selves. Someone had been handing out some lovely green gummies . . .

'Oh no! Not here as well,' said Pearlin. 'The whole world's gone wobbly!'

Then she saw someone waving a flag from the top of the library. Mac n Cheese circled around the library to get a closer look. It was Argie, the young librarian cyclops, one of Catalogue's best friends.

'Hey there!' Argie shouted. 'Any chance of a lift out of here?'

Pearlin brought Mac n Cheese in to land on the top of the library.

'Happy to fly you away,'

said Pearlin. 'But first I could really do with some help finding a book or two. I need to know everything there is to know about slime magic.'

Argie held up a very thin green book.

'I had the same idea,' he said. 'And this thousand year old book is all I could find. Now, if you don't mind, I'd really love it if we could go now.'

Just then the door to the roof burst open and a crowd of see-through green people spilled out on to the roof.

'Come and have a gummy!' they said as one.

'Hop on,' said Pearlin to Argie and they launched into the air.

'Let's find somewhere where we're not gonna be bothered,' said Pearlin and turned Mac n Cheese towards the Jabby Mountains.

CHAPTER 37

It's not easy to find somewhere to land in the Jabby Mountains. The Jabby Mountains are very pointy and . . . well, jabby.

Finally, Mac n Cheese found a jutting piece of rock high on Mount Prong and landed very delicately. Pearlin took out her telescope and looked out at the wide landscape below them. From all corners of Squirrel Helm she could see people (slightly green and wobbly) walking north. It looked like they were heading towards Castle Sideways.

'The books says they're slime-drones,' explained Argie. 'People controlled by slime magic. They're fed some slime and their bodies start to make lots of it. Then a slime sorcerer can drain it and use it for themselves!'

'Ugh!' said Pearlin. 'Sounds horrible.'

They settled down to read more. Mac n Cheese kept a look out. They also kept Pearlin and Archie warm by starting a little fire.

Archie read the book out loud to Pearlin.

THE RARE SCIENCE OF SLIME MAGIC
By Grendella Granit, a Sorcerer

Slime, also known as slayme or sloom to the old ones, is a tricksy magic. Few can master it, for it is slippery and oozy and icky. Only I and my good friend Baron Alan of Blunder have had any success in understanding it.

Unlike other magic, to become a slime magician, you must become the source of the magic yourself! You must become a sorcerer of slime!

One great advantage is that slime creatures are very hard to destroy. You may be able to live for a very, very long time! The great disadvantage is that you will look like a great, big, disgusting bogey. It may, of course, be possible to reshape yourself for a while into something that looks human or animal. But doing so would take years to master.

Turning yourself into a slime sorcerer is not at all easy. One must use the essential ingredient at just the perfect ripeness.

Pearlin said, 'I bet this essential ingredient is gonna turn out to be some kind of stupid vegetable like a potato or parsnip or a cucumber, ain't it?'

Argie read aloud, 'The essential ingredient is . . . er . . . corn-on-the-cob!'

Pearlin nodded. 'Told yer. Sweetcorn. Who knew that was magic!'

'Well, it can magically pass through the body without changing much,' said Argie thoughtfully.

'True,' agreed Pearlin. 'That is kinda magic, I suppose.'

The corn must be fully yellow before used. Any greenness left in the corn will make the slime evil! I have told this to Baron Alan of Blunder, but he doubts me. This is most worrisome.

Sadly, I cannot harness this magic myself as I am an ogre. My stone skeleton repels the slime and try as I might, I cannot become a sorcerer of slime.

If you are interested in becoming a slime sorcerer, you can find below the many ingredients needed. Also, you will need to follow the very very very complicated recipe!

Pearlin took the book and looked through the ingredients and the magical recipe.

'Is it any help?' asked Argie.

'Yeah,' said Pearlin, looking a little worried. 'I know exactly where all these ingredients are. And where all the stuff is to turn me into a slime sorcerer. Trouble is . . . it's in my laboratory in

Castle Sideways. And that's not the nicest place right now.'

'So should we just give up and live up here for the rest of our lives?' asked Argie hopefully.

'Sorry Argie. Not happening. It's time to fly!'

CHAPTER 38

Now, who remembers where Knight Sir Louis was at the end of Chapter 34?

The Eldogre strode out of the forest of Tumblin' Klatterbang and into the land of Blunder (also known as Blunderland). She carried Louis, Catalogue, Wurt and the other ogres in her huge hand.

The small country of Blunderland was a wide and breezy grassland. A few animals grazed there, but there were no obvious houses, and no people to be seen. In the middle of it all was a castle.

'Castle Blunder, at last,' said Louis with a chuckle. 'To think this is where I was heading. Not much to defend here.'

The Eldogre set them down in front of the castle beside a vending machine.

A VENDING MACHINE?

YEAH. YOU KNOW. FOR CRISPS, POP AND SNACKS AND STUFF.

DO WE HAVE THOSE HERE?

OF COURSE, WHERE DO YOU THINK I GOT THIS PACKET OF DRIED MOUSE EARS FROM?

Louis stepped forward to look at it. 'Well, that's not what you expect to find in a vending machine.'

Catalogue chuckled and said, 'It's Mysto!'

Petunia peered in. 'What's a Mysto? Looks like a little man with a funny beard. And lots of nose hair.'

'Ugh!' said Moss.
'Who'd want to vend that?'

Catalogue was already putting in a penny and pressing the button.

TIME FREEZING VENDING MACHINE

There was a SHUSSSH and a KORRRRRR and a PLOK! And the machine door opened and Mysto fell out with a CLONK. He appeared to be frozen solid.

'Here we go,' said the Eldogre picking up his frozen body. **'I met this little wizentor centuries ago. He said that one day a boy called Louis would come looking for him. And then he got inside this machine he made and froze himself in time. I'd forgotten about it until you said your name.'**

She breathed over him with warm air, then set him down in front of Louis. The ice crust over Mysto cracked a little and he blinked.

'Louis? Is that you? Ah! At last, I'm back from the past!' said Mysto.

The dwarfish wizard shook off the ice and brushed himself down. He was the same old Mysto. A cheery smile. Piercing amber eyes. And a lot of nose hair.

'What happened to you?' Louis asked Mysto. 'The last I saw of you, you sniffed all that time pepper and vanished!'

'Where'd you go?' asked Catalogue.

'And when?' asked Louis.

'Prepare yourself for a very long story,' said Mysto.

'Maybe just give us the headlines,' suggested Louis.

'Or just skip to the end?' said Catalogue.

CHAPTER 39

After Mysto had accidentally snorted up his time pepper (see Chapter 18 for details), he'd found himself a thousand years in the past.

Later, he wrote all about his time travelling adventures in a very long and complicated series of books entitled *Mysto's Baffling Odyssey Roving In Nature's Garden.*

Otherwise known as Mysto's B.O.R.I.N.G. books for short.

To cut a long story short:

Mysto spent a long time roaming through the olden days, and was finally ready to come back to his own time. But how? He'd lost the time pepper when he'd sneezed into it.

Eventually he came to the land of Tumblin' Klatterbang and met the ogrish wizard, Grendella Granit. They became firm friends, but she was unable to help. She had mostly given up magic. Too many things could go wrong with it, she explained. But she pointed Mysto to the nearby kingdom of Blunderland. Her old partner Baron Alan lived there and was still trying to perfect a new kind of magic – slime magic.

Mysto went to see him.

Baron Alan wasn't as nice as Grendella.

'I hear you are a wizard, like me,' said Mysto, hoping to bond.

Baron Alan scoffed. 'I doubt you're anything like me. I'm about to become the greatest wizard in history!' And he pointed to a large cauldron full of bubbling liquid.

'Are you making soup?' asked Mysto. 'I love soup.'

'Of course not,' barked the baron. 'I'm about to turn myself into the world's first slime sorcerer and this is the potion. All I need to add is a corn-on-the-cob and it's ready!'

He reached for an unripe, very green head of corn.

'Wouldn't a nice yellow one be better?' Mysto suggested.

'Shut up!' said Baron Alan, throwing in the green corn and taking a sip of his slime soup.

In a few moments
the baron's whole
body wobbled
and he turned
into a green,
slimy blob.

'HA HA!' he shouted. 'I
am now a sorcerer of slime
and I will live forever!
I will grow to become
the most powerful wizard ever, ever!'

'Er, I think you must have made a mistake with
your recipe,' said Mysto. 'Perhaps the green corn?'

It was true, because the baron was shrinking.
He'd been a man. Then a man-sized blob. But
soon he was no bigger than a lump of snot.

'AGH! No matter,' said Baron Alan, his voice becoming fainter as he got smaller and smaller. 'I will find a way to grow . . . even if it takes me a thousand years! I will become all powerful! People will fear me! I will be known as Acidic Alan! Or the Acidic Baron! Or Baron Slime! I'm not sure yet. HA HA!'

And he slid off through the blades of grass . . .

. . . away from his castle . . .

. . . to take over the world.

Very slowly.

Mysto realised the Baron wasn't going to help him travel back to the future. Sometimes you just have to do things yourself. Fortunately, the baron had left behind a wizarding workshop full of useful kit. So Mysto made himself a vending machine and froze himself for a thousand years.

TIME FREEZING VENDING MACHINE

CHAPTER 40

Louis considered Mysto's story and said, 'I really must try time travel one of these days!'

'It's not all sniffing roses and stuff,' said Catalogue, who'd had her own time travel adventure. 'Specially if yous end up in the old dinosaur ages around dinner-time.'

'Well, I don't think there's anything to worry about,' said Mysto, 'because I don't think this Acidic Alan ever came to anything much.'

'I'm not so sure about that,' said Louis.

And just then, a bottle flew in!

Catalogue scratched her head, looking confused. 'Scuse me, Louis, but is it normals for drinks to come flying up to you these days?'

'It's a Thinking Drink,' explained Louis. 'I asked Pearlin to send it to me.'

'Let's hope it's not curdled,' said Mysto. 'I once drank a Thinking Drink that had spent too much time in the sun. I spent a lot of time thinking in the toilet after that.'

'No, it's good,' said Louis. 'And it worked. Here come her thoughts . . . Aha! Pearlin discovered something nasty in the gummies. I knew it!'

'And I'm beginning to wonder if Acidic Alan is, at last, ready to take over the world.'

'You've met him?' said Mysto.

'I think so,' said Louis. 'If I'm right, he was in disguise and using a different name . . . Sir Lyme!'

DUN DUN DURRRRRRR

THAT WOULD EXPLAIN HIS SLIMY PERSONALITY

AND HIS GREEN EYES

OI! I'VE GOT GREEN EYES!

CHAPTER 41

Louis knew he had to return to Castle Sideways as soon as possible. He had to face Lyme and defeat him. But how?

'**The ogres will help you,**' said the Eldogre. '**Slime magic doesn't work on us.**'

'Ah, that explains why Sir Lyme hates ogres so much,' said Louis.

'Hey Eldogrey wotsit,' said Catalogue. 'How comes yous has heard of slime magicals?'

'**Well, you see,**' said the Eldogre, '**When I was younger and smaller, I dabbled in magic myself.**'

234

'OH!' said Mysto, realising where he'd met her before. 'I met you a thousand years ago didn't I? You're Grendella Granit!'

'That's me,' said the Eldogre. **'Or it was.'**

'Then you should come with us,' said Louis.

'Sadly, I cannot,' she yawned. **'Soon, it's time for me to sleep again. But . . . I can offer you something to take with you.'**

And she reached up to her head and felt around for something there.

'Ah, here it is,' she said.

She brought down a sword made entirely from a single piece of stone. Its blade and hilt were rough and textured.

'Something I made when I was still practising magic,' she said, and laid it before Louis.

'Oooo!' said Mysto, impressed. 'Does it have a name? Magic swords must have a super cool name.'

'Yes!' said the Eldogre. **'This sword is called . . . Chris!'**

'You're pulling my trotters, right?' said Catalogue, unimpressed. 'We's already got a sword called Dave. What's the next one going to be – John?'

'Chris has the power to turn things to stone,' explained the Eldgore, **'though it's not easy to use I'm afraid. You'll have to practise the special flick to make it work.'**

Then the huge ogre gave a big yawn, lay down around the ruins of Castle Blunder and fell fast asleep.

Louis looked down at the sword.

He thought to himself: *I already have a sword. I don't need another one. And I don't think Catalogue or Mysto would want this thing. So, who should have it?*

He looked across at Wurt and remembered his book about Knight Sir David 523rd, the story of an heroic ogre.

'Wurt, a few days ago I was told I should have a squire. I didn't really want one. But now I think I've found the ideal person. Would you like to take up the sword Chris, and be Squire Wurt of Tumblin' Klatterbang?'

Wurt looked at Louis, amazed. 'Me?'

'Great ideas,' agreed Catalogue. 'Welcome to the team, squire!'

'Better pick it up,' said Mysto. 'It's your sword now.'

Wurt stepped forward, leaned down, put both hands around the sword and lifted it high above

him in a heroic pose.

And fell over backwards because it was amazingly heavy.

CHAPTER 42

Pearlin had returned to Castle Sideways. Well, sort of. She and Argie were flying around on Mac n Cheese, high above the castle.

They were hiding amongst the clouds, because down below the grassy plain surrounding the castle was full of people. They had come from across the kingdom and beyond. Squire Lyme had travelled far and wide handing out his gummies. And all these people had eaten them and become green oozy slime-drones!

'We're gonna have to find a way to sneak in,' said Pearlin.

Argie looked around at the clouds. 'Perhaps we could ride in under cover of fog?'

'Oo! Nice one, Argie,' said Pearlin and she leaned over and whispered in Mac n Cheese's ears.

A moment later, Mac n Cheese took two deep breaths and breathed out not fire . . . but steam! They spiralled down to the castle below, hiding themselves in the steamy fog.

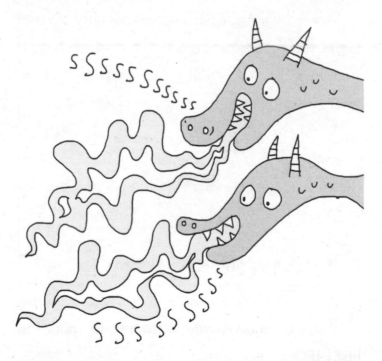

At last, they came to the entrance to Pearlin's lab and quietly slipped inside.

Luckily enough there was no one there, and Pearlin got to work straight away. She took out Grendella Granit's book and checked the spell page.

'Right! Time to make some slime magic of my own,' she said.

Meanwhile, Argie peered with his one large eye out of the window. He could see the slime-drones stretching on for miles. There was a massive gormless army of them!

'What are they waiting for?' he wondered aloud.

And just then, he saw a very tall man, as tall as three men, stride down from the castle.

'Who's that?' wondered Argie and Pearlin came over.

It was Sir Lyme and trailing behind him, dragging her heels, was the witch Hagatha Squint.

'Blimey,' said Pearlin. 'What's he done to himself? He's massive!'

The giant Sir Lyme approached the crowd of slime-drones.

'Ah! At last!' he said. 'I am so very tired of holding this human form. It is time to be ME again!'

He uttered a spell and it echoed across the plain and the slime-drones swayed like a field of grass in the wind.

URGLE FLURGLE WIBBLE WOBBLE SPLOINK

And with that, Sir Lyme oozed and squirmed. He seemed to melt!

'What's happening to him?' said Argie, worried.

'Looks like he's returning to his true shape,' said Pearlin, fascinated.

Sure enough, the features of Sir Lyme were soon gone completely. He turned greener, wobblier and

see-through. He turned into a huge green blob. A
Sorcerer of Slime. Acidic Alan.

CHAPTER 43

Acidic Alan, three times the height of a normal man, bright green and transparent, slid forward towards his slime-drones. They looked up at him in wonder.

'Ahem,' said a voice behind him and he swivelled his slimy body to look. It was Hagatha Squint.

'What is it, apprentice?' said Alan tetchily. His voice was still like Sir Lyme's but a little deeper, and wobblier than before.

'Just wondering if now's a good time for you to make me a slime creature too. You know, cos I've been waiting for ages.'

'Patience!' said Alan. 'Your time will come.'

'Right,' said Hagatha, before saying under her breath, 'sure it will.'

She folded her arms and sulked, while Alan raised his slimy arms to his minions.

'Come forward all and give me your slime!'

One by one the people in the crowd stepped forward and Alan absorbed their slime. And each time the slime sorcerer grew larger. And each slime-drone would then suddenly be normal and human again.

One of the ex-slime-drones turned out to be Bonnie Smashington the tea shop manager from Nervous Klench.

'Oh, what happened to me?' she wondered, then turned to the lady next to her. It was Hagatha Squint.

'Are you alright, dear?' Bonnie asked Hagatha. 'You seem rather glum.'

'I don't think my master is ever going to make me into a slimeball,' said Hagatha sadly.

'That sounds like a good thing, doesn't it?' suggested Bonnie.

'You wouldn't understand,' said Hagatha.

'Well, no,' said Bonnie, 'though I wouldn't mind turning into a large currant bun filled with strawberry jam. So I understand a little bit.'

Above in the castle, Argie and Pearlin watched with horror as Acidic Alan grew and grew and grew.

'I think that might be the most disgusting thing I've ever clapped eyes on,' Pearlin said.

'What are we going to do?' asked Argie, quivering.

'Work faster!' said Pearlin.

She rushed back and gathered all the pots, pans, potions, lotions, powders and chowders that she needed for her own slime magic recipe. But one thing was missing.

'I need some corn-on-the-cob,' she said, turning to Argie who was hiding under a large pan. 'How do you fancy popping to the kitchen for me?'

CHAPTER 44

Across the country in Blunderland, Louis prepared to leave for Castle Sideways. He climbed aboard Clunkie with Catalogue. Wurt took the inside compartment.

Mysto had rustled up some new wings for Clunkalot from parts of the vending machine.

'I promise these ones won't fly off on their own,' he said.

'But won't three of us be too heavy for you, Clunkie?' asked Catalogue.

Clunkie neighed, flapped his newly fixed wings and printed out a haiku.

CARRYING MY FRIENDS
IS LIKE THE VASTNESS OF SPACE
THERE'S NOTHING TO IT

'Oo! Very poetic,' said Catalogue.

'What about you, Mysto?' asked Louis. 'How will you get to Castle Sideways?'

'I'll come along with our ogre friends here,' Mysto said. And he indicated Acorn, Moss and Petunia.

'But it'll take us ages to march all the way!' Petunia said.

'Yes, well maybe I can invent a speedy potion or something,' suggested Mysto. 'It'll be like we're all on fast forward.'

'Sounds fun,' said Acorn.

'Does it?' wondered Moss.

'We'll see you there!' said Louis impatiently. And Knight Sir Louis, Squire Wurt of Tumblin' Klatterbang and Henrietta Catalogue launched into the air and headed for Castle Sideways.

But first, they made a stop at Chivalry Farm to drop in on Louis' parents. The slime-drones had been trying to invade the farm to hand out gummies so Champion Trixie and the gnomes were very keen to march on Castle Sideways too. Though Louis' dad Ned decided to remain at the farm and protect the farm animals.

'Don't worry,' Ned said. 'I've been tinkering with that giant damsel robot head and I think I've got it working again. I found an evil potato powering the brain so I replaced it with a nice egg. It can't talk any more, but it can cluck and squawk.'

'BOK BOK BOK BOKARK'

'And one of the gnomes found this,' said Louis' mum. 'You might want to return it to Mysto now he's reappeared!' She held out Mysto's time pepper pot. 'He must have dropped it when he vanished. There's not much of it left.'

Louis took it and shook the few grains inside. 'More trouble than it's worth, if you ask me,' he said and stored it safely inside Clunkie.

After a hearty dinner, Louis and his friends flew off once more making their way towards Castle Sideways.

'So Louis,' said Catalogue, 'hows we gonna defeat a nasty old slime sorcerer?'

'I've got a few ideas up my metal sleeve,' Louis said, thinking. 'But the biggest advantage we have is that Lyme or Acidic Alan, or whatever he wants to call himself, doesn't think children like me can do anything much.'

Just then, Wurt opened the hatch on the side of Clunkie and peered out.

'Scuse me.' said Wurt. 'I'm feeling a bit siii—' And then he threw up.

CHAPTER 45

Back in Squirrel Helm, Argie was sneaking around Castle Sideways looking for the kitchens. He had never been to the castle before. You might think he'd struggle to find his way around, but you'd be wrong. Because Argie was a librarian. That meant he was not only well-read, but was very good at finding things.

ABLE TO FIND YOU THE BOOK YOU NEED ACCORDING TO TITLE, AUTHOR, COLOUR OF COVER, SMELL OF BOOK, FEEL OF THE PAGES...

LIBRARIAN OF THE MONTH

He had also read 'A Walking Tour of Castles by Knight Sir Astrid' which was so detailed that Argie felt like he'd been to Castle Sideways before.

He sneaked quietly and quickly towards the kitchens. All he needed was one corn-on-the-cob. He had to find it without being spotted. But it wasn't easy. Slimy castle courtiers were sliding around everywhere. But at last, he found his way into the kitchen and hid behind the cool store. There were two cooks in there, also slime-drones.

'What is it . . . you know . . . when there's bits of raw food . . . in a bowl . . . and stuff,' said one cook to the other.

'Errrrrrrrrrrrrrrr . . . salad?' said the other dreamily.

'Yes. That's it. Let's make a . . . um . . . what was it?'

'What's what?'

Argie opened up the cool store, chucked a few vegetables into a bowl and pushed the bowl along the table towards the two cooks.

'Hello . . . Who made this?' said one cook.

'Looks like a . . . thingy . . . you know . . . salad,' said the second.

'Oo . . . Did you make this?'

'Must have done! Come . . . on . . .' said the second.

And they both took hold of the dish and oozed out of the room.

'Phew!' said Argie to himself. 'Now. Time to find some corn.'

He returned to the cool store. There were all kinds of vegetables jumbled together.

'Come on, come on Argie!' he said to himself. 'Just one corn-on-the-cob! Just one! Then we can stop the slime!'

'And what's so special about corn-on-the-cob?' said someone and Argie jumped with surprise, banging his head.

'OW!'

He turned. Hagatha Squint was standing there, her wand pointed directly at him.

'Uh-oh,' said Argie.

CHAPTER 46

Wurt had been sick in mid-air but was finally feeling better. Clunkalot had come into land in the valley below so he could recover.

'Sorry, Wurt,' said Louis. 'We shouldn't have flown off straight after lunch.'

'It's not that,' said Wurt nervously. 'It's just it's all so sudden. Becoming a squire. Running off to do battle. I don't feel ready! I don't even know how to use a normal sword, never mind a big magic stony one.'

'You're right,' said Louis. 'I made you a squire but haven't trained you how to actually be one.'

'Maybes we should have a little old sword practice, right here,' suggested Catalogue.

'Yes,' said Louis, 'but I'm not sure we have time. Hey! Time!'

Then he laughed and clanked his helmet with his gauntlet.

'Of course, we have time!'

And he retrieved the time pepper from Clunkie's storage.

'We only need a couple of grains each,' and he unscrewed the top. 'Nobody sneeze, alright?'

He gave a couple of dark pepper grains to Catalogue, Wurt, Clunkie and reserved two for himself.

'Here we go. Eat up!'

They ate up.

They vanished.

And then reappeared two weeks earlier in the same spot.

'Right then,' said Louis. 'Let's get training!'

Two weeks might sound like a long time.

To become a great knight takes months, even years. But two weeks was better than nothing. After two weeks training, Wurt could handle his sword Chris, but he'd only mastered the basic moves. And he really struggled with the special magical flick. How was that supposed to work? He couldn't get it to turn anything into stone.

'It's no good,' he said at last.

The two weeks were nearly up. They had almost returned to the moment when they'd travelled back in time.

'I think you'll have to go without me,' Wurt said.

'Don't be giving up,' said Catalogue.

'I think maybe I just like writing stories about knights,' said Wurt worriedly. 'I'm not brave enough to be one.'

'You were brave enough to face the Eldogre,' said Louis.

'Yeah,' said Catalogue, 'plus think about all them amazing story ideas yous is gonna get from fighting a slime sorcererererer.'

'That's true, I suppose,' agreed Wurt.

'And if we defeats the big old blob,' continued Catalogue, 'you'll be totally famous and everyone'll love you and then they'll want to buy all your books.'

'You think so?' said Wurt.
'I hadn't thought of that!'

He leapt up and grabbed his sword Chris.

'I need to think of this differently,' Wurt said aloud. 'If I was writing about a magic sword, what would I do?'

Suddenly, he had an idea. He stood in his most heroic pose, flicked his sword until it pointed straight up in the air and said, 'By the Power of Tumblin' Klatterbang!'

A moment later a lightning bolt struck the sword and Chris the sword glowed like a star.

'YEAH!' shouted Louis.

Wurt looked at it amazed and touched a nearby

tree stump. The stump immediately turned to stone and the sword's light vanished.

'WOW!' said Wurt. 'It worked!'

'Yeah, but next time maybe give us a warning,' said Catalogue. 'I don't want to be standing so close.'

Wurt and Louis turned to look at her. The static from the electricity had made her hair stand on end. And her lovely ruff, once light and made of lace, was now solid granite.

COR, THIS RUFF
IS RIGHT HEAVY.

CHAPTER 47

Argie arrived back in Pearlin's lab holding a bright yellow corn-on-the-cob.

'Back already Argie,' said Pearlin. 'Nice work!' She had followed the recipe precisely and now her slime potion was well on its way to being finished. It had indeed been very very very complicated. She'd almost used stink root instead of stink leaves, she'd almost added the cornflakes before the dragon's earwax, and almost stirred it all with a wooden spoon instead of an old shoe. Close one!

But then she saw that Argie didn't look quite right. He was walking in stiffly. Hagatha followed behind with Argie at wand-point.

'Hello Pearlin, what are we up to here?'

'None of your business, Hagatha,' said Pearlin.
'Just saving the world. Again.'

Hagatha stepped up close to Pearlin's book and
looked at the title.

She read aloud: 'The Rare Science of Slime
Magic, by Grendella Granit.' Then looked at
Pearlin in wonder, 'Is this what I think it is?'

Suddenly, there was a huge, roaring, gurgling
chuckle.

They all raced to the window. Outside, Acidic
Alan was larger still. The huge army of slime-
drones continued to come forward and give up

their slime. People had come from all over the Many Kingdoms – from Hogford, from Nervous Klench, from Portly Wishwash . . . everywhere.

'More MORE MORE!' Acidic Alan shouted.

'What is his problem?' wondered Pearlin aloud. 'Why is he so greedy?'

'I think he just wants to be noticed,' said Hagatha sadly. 'Don't we all, duck. I wanted him to notice me, but . . .' She sighed heavily.

Pearlin looked over at Mac n Cheese who had been sleeping in the corner. They had woken and were now in prime position to roast Hagatha. But Pearlin shook her head at them.

Instead, she turned to Hagatha and said, 'Right. It's time to make a choice. You can stand here pointing that wand at us or you can make yourself useful and pass me the owl tears from that cupboard. What's it gonna be?'

CHAPTER 48

In Chapter 48 we're wondering about King Burt. How's he doing? What's he up to? Here he is with his butler.

I'm glad we stopped by in Chapter 48. King
Burt is coming to his senses at last. Phew.

CHAPTER 49

Okay. I think this is it folks. We're about to do the final battle. Let's just take a moment to breathe and stay calm. Let's all listen to the Bunny of Relaxation.

Hi there.
I am the Bunny of Relaxtion.
I want you to use your calmest voice when
reading this.

Breathe in.
Deeply.
Imagine that the air is filling up every part of
your body.

Breathe out.
Slowly.
Imagine that all the tightness is leaving your body.

Now, imagine . . .
. . . that you have an enormous juicy carrot
and some delicious dandelion leaves
and that your tummy is rumbling.

Oh . . . hang on. I think I might be hungry.
Sorry, you'll have to relax on your own.
Bye!

Let's try something else. Maybe draw yourself some cute pictures of bunnies here or something.

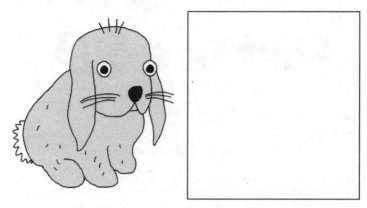

Draw your bunny here

Okay? Ready? Let's do this!

CHAPTER 50

At last, Acidic Alan had absorbed all the slime he could get. He was no longer just a giant. He was gargantuan! Taller than Castle Sideways hill. A huge, towering mass of green slime!

'Finally, I am all powerful!' said Alan. 'It has taken me soooooooo long! A thousand boring, slow, tedious years!'

The people who had come from across the Many Kingdoms were slime-free at last and walking around in confusion.

HOW DID WE GET HERE?

MY LEGS ARE SO TIRED. LIKE I'VE BEEN WALKING AND WALKING

ER HAS ANYONE ELSE NOTICED THE GIANT SLIME MONSTER?

Acidic Alan was now so tall he could see for miles and miles in every direction.

'All of the world will be mine! Ruled over by me and me alone!'

He'll probably laugh now. Loudly. Because that's what baddies do, isn't it?

HA HA HA HA HA HA HA HA HA

Told you.

But it didn't last long because just then, something came soaring out of the clouds down towards Acidic Alan and Castle Sideways.

It was Knight Sir Louis riding Clunkalot with Catalogue and Wurt sat behind him.

'Cor blimey,' said Catalogue. 'He's got a tiny weeny bit bigger than he was a thousand years ago.'

Knight Sir Louis preferred to have time to come up with a plan to defeat a nasty enemy. Sometimes he had days to work out an intricate scheme. Sometimes an afternoon with friends, spitballing ideas. But today, he had about three seconds.

'Get ready with your sword, Wurt,' said Louis. 'Hopefully it can turn something that big to stone.'

HEY LYME!
ALAN! WHATEVER!
PREPARE TO DO
BATTLE!

'Ready as I'll ever be,' muttered a worried Wurt.

'We'll keep him distracted,' said Louis, 'and you can do your thing while he's looking the other way.'

Acidic Alan looked up at them, saw Louis and sneered. 'Oh no,' he mocked, 'the little boy's back. I'm so afraid.'

And he raised a finger and a huge jet of green slime flew towards Clunkalot.

SPLURRRGGEE

Clunkie folded his wings and dropped like a stone, the jet of slime missing him by inches.

'Great job, Clunkie—' started Louis.

But Alan had fired again from his other finger. Another jet of slime slopped into Clunkalot, sending Louis and his friends flying. They crashed into the ground below but had a soft sticky landing.

'I'm sure you're used to winning these battles, boy,' sneered Alan. 'But you've never met someone with my power before!' Alan let out two great streams of slime into the huge crowd of people. The flood of slime gathered them up and sent them all oozing and slopping away from the castle.

'Real power! AT LAST!' said Alan. And then he did some more evil laughing. You know, ha ha ha etcetera.

Louis' Instant Plan A had already gone a bit wrong. But Louis knew there was still a whole alphabet to work through. So Instant Plan B went into action. What was it? Even Louis didn't know yet.

CHAPTER 51.

Louis and Catalogue picked themselves up and helped clear the slime off each other. They looked around for the others and saw Clunkie pulling Wurt out of the sticky gloop nearby.

'What's the plan?' said Catalogue.

'The plan was not to get hit with slime so quickly,' said Louis. 'But too late for that now.'

Above them, they heard a whistle. They looked up.

Pearlin was waving at them from her window. 'Oi! Louis! Up here!'

'Pearlin! She's here and she's alright,' said Louis, waving at her. 'OK. New plan. Catalogue, you keep Alan distracted. I'm going to see Pearlin.'

And he ran off towards the castle.

'Oh yeah,' complained Catalogue. 'Just keeps a massive blob of evil slime busy. What could go wrong-a-long? Ha!' But even though she didn't much like the idea, she also knew that Louis was good at making plans . . . and making them up quickly. So Catalogue trotted over to Alan and shouted up at him.

'Eh! Alan! I want a word with you!'

Acidic Alan looked around for the voice and then down at Catalogue.

'What is this?' he said. 'A talking pig?'

'I ain't a piggywig. I is a boar.'

'What do you want, small boar?' Acidic Alan asked, bending down towards the tiny, hairy figure far below him.

'Well,' said Catalogue, 'I never met no one like you before. I once met a whiffy wizard who wanted to be a king and that. Loved telling everyone whats to do. And I met a whopping dragon who liked setting fire to . . . well, everything. Loved a bit of chaos. So I is wondering . . . why is it you wanting all this power? What's it all for?'

'What for?' said Alan. 'Well, I want power because . . .'

And he stopped. Because he'd spent so long working out *how* to obtain power, he'd never actually thought about *why* he wanted it.

'Er. Because, then, er, I, can, er, you know,

er . . . be power . . . ful,' said Alan looking a little confused.

Meanwhile, Louis raced up to Pearlin's laboratory. He had to leapfrog a few slime-drones on his way. When he knocked, he was surprised to discover Hagatha Squint opening the door for him.

'Alright, me duck,' said Hagatha, cheerfully.

'What's going on?' said Louis.

'You've arrived at the crucial moment,' said Pearlin. 'Watch this!'

Louis looked over to see Pearlin holding a perfect yellow corn-on-the-cob over a boiling pot of slimy potion.

'And three, two, one . . .'

She let the corn drop into the potion.

PLOP!

At the same time outside, Clunkalot had finally pulled Wurt out of the slime. Clunkie flicked out his new wings and tried flapping them. They still worked. Wurt climbed on Clunkie's back and felt for his magic sword Chris. He looked around at the scene of chaos. Louis was nowhere to be seen. Catalogue was talking to the slime sorcerer.

Wurt swallowed nervously. 'I'm not sure I can do this, Clunkie.'

Clunkalot decided to give Wurt a boost. So, he wrote him a poem.

THERE ONCE WAS AN OGRE CALLED WURT
WHO WAS MADE FROM A CRYSTAL CALLED CHERT
HE WENT FROM A ZERO
RIGHT UP TO A HERO
WHEN FIGHTING A SLIMY OLD SQUIRT

'Oh wow!' said Wurt. 'Poetry. Yes. That's it. A little story. I need to tell myself a little story. Er . . .

ONCE UPON A TIME, THERE WAS A LITTLE BRAVE OGRE WITH A MAGIC SWORD. THE OGRE DIDN'T HAVE MUCH, BUT HE DID HAVE AN IMAGINATION. AND ON THIS DAY, HE IMAGINED THAT HE WASN'T TERRIFIED OF FIGHTING GIGANTIC GREEN WIZARDS. HE IMAGINED HE WAS A GREAT STONE WARRIOR CARVED FROM A MOUNTAINSIDE! YEAH! A HERO! A LEGEND! AND AN AUTHOR OF BOOKS YOU FOUND IN ACTUAL SHOPS!

It had worked. Sort of. Wurt felt just a tiny bit braver.

'Right then Clunkie,' he said, 'looks like it's down to us. It's time to turn Alan to stone!'

CHAPTER 52

Clunkalot flapped his wings and he and Wurt flew into the air.

Acidic Alan didn't notice because Catalogue was still keeping him busy.

'You're right, pig-thing,' said Alan to Catalogue. 'I need to work out what to do with all this power.'

'Maybe you can be all fluffy and nice,' suggested Catalogue. 'A big slimy blob like you could be popular at parties. Doing jokes. Making kids snortle.'

'Make children laugh!' barked Alan. 'I don't even *like* children. Especially when they're laughing at me. When I was young, I remember being laughed at by all the other children.'

'That sounds like a sad old memory,' said Catalogue. 'Want to talk about it? Might help work out why you've gone all nasty.'

'NO! I do not want to talk about it!' said Alan, suddenly furious. 'I don't like children, I don't much like adults and NOW I DON'T THINK I LIKE PIGS EITHER!'

'Boars,' corrected Catalogue.

'SHUT UP!' said Alan. 'I know what I'm going to do with all this power. I'm going to cover the whole world in slime. An entire planet of slime. And me the only thing on it. That's what I'm going to do!'

'Sounds a bit rubbish to me,' said Catalogue honestly.

Meanwhile, up in the air, Wurt was preparing himself for the attack. He held on tight to Clunkalot

while awkwardly lifting up his magical stone sword.

'Here goes nothing,' said Wurt to himself, raising the sword above his head. 'By the power of . . . WHOA!'

Lifting the sword properly in mid-flight was impossible. He lost his balance and the sword Chris fell from his hand. It plunged downwards, straight into Alan's blobby body.

'Oo!' said big slimey Alan, feeling a tiny pinprick as the sword hit him. He looked up and saw Wurt on Clunkalot. 'Ugh! An ogre. I hate ogres!'

He fired off a splat of slime in the air. This time Clunkalot managed to spin out of the way and fly round the back of Castle Sideways.

Meanwhile, Catalogue watched as Chris the sword slowly slowly sunk down inside Alan until it arrived on the ground. The sword didn't seem to hurt Alan at all; one of the advantages of being immortal and made of slime, Catalogue supposed.

'Not going to be much fun, trying to get that back,' Catalogue said to herself.

Just then there was a fanfare of trumpets and the beat of drums. Acidic Alan rotated his slimy body to see what it was. He was getting super annoyed with all these minor distractions. First, there had been that child knight, then the hairy pig, and then the little ogre on a horse. Now what?

Heading straight for the castle were two bands of warriors. The first was Champion Trixie, leading General Gnomus and his gnomes. The second band were ogres led by Mysto and included Acorn, Petunia and Moss.

'Hey Alan! Now's a nice time to say let's all be friends and stuff,' Catalogue suggested.

'No! Now's the time ... the TIME FOR SLIME!' said Alan.

'Fair enough,' said Catalogue and she hurried off to the castle. 'I hope Louis' sorted out this new plan by now. Or things is about to get right sticky.'

CHAPTER 53

Louis had looked out of Pearlin's window and seen Wurt lose his sword and Catalogue make a (very sensible) run for it. Things were clearly not going their way. But he also saw his mum, Mysto, the gnomes and the ogres arriving to join the fight.

'If we're going to defeat Acidic Alan, we're going to need all the help we can get,' Louis said to Pearlin.

'Exactly why I made this,' she explained, pointing at the cauldron.

'Fight slime with slime, you mean?' said Louis, looking in. 'Interesting. And probably very messy.' The slime potion smelled awful. It was gloopy and a sickly yellow.

'You're sure this is how it's supposed to look and smell?' said Louis doubtfully.

'It was a very very very complicated recipe,' said Pearlin. 'But I followed it to the letter.'

'Whoever drinks it,' said Hagatha dreamily, 'will become a slime sorcerer.'

'Yeah, but who'd want to,' said Louis, feeling sick. 'It's got a skin on top like cold custard. Ugh!'

'Yeah, it's pretty grim,' agreed Pearlin.

'What are you two talking about?' said Hagatha. 'It's beautiful!' And she took a big sniff of the stinky potion.

'Who's gonna drink the potion?' Pearlin asked

290

Louis. 'You or me? Who's gonna be the slime sorcerer?'

Louis considered the option. The upside was that you became a slime magician and lived forever. The downside was that you turned into a sort of slimy bogey thing.

'I'll do it if I have to,' he said, 'but surely you should drink it, Pearlin. You're a wizard after all. It's your sort of thing.'

'I like being a wizard,' said Pearlin. 'But I also like being me.'

'So who's it going to be?' said Louis desperately.

Beside them, Hagatha was happily stirring the liquid with a shoe and saying, 'Who's a lovely pot of slime then. Coochee coochee coo.'

Pearlin and Louis looked at each other and nodded. Suddenly, it was pretty obvious who the new slime sorcerer should be.

'Hagatha,' said Louis. 'Your moment has come.'

And he gathered up some of the potion and handed it to her.

'For me?' said Hagatha in wonder.

'Right! I have an idea,' said Louis.

Catalogue came running in and said, 'Cor. It's totally nutzoid out there. How's plan B, C, D or whatever coming along?'

Louis quickly ran through his new plan. He spoke really fast.

'OkayweneedtodistractAlananywaywecanwhileIhelpWurtgethisswordbackIseveryoneready?'

'YES!' said his friends.

'Then let's go!' said Louis and they all ran out to join the battle once more.

Catalogue was right. It was totally nutzoid.

Acidic Alan was fighting single-handed against the host of ogres and gnomes. He fired off spurts of slime in every direction. He made slime into boxing gloves, tentacles and giant boots, and punched, grabbed and kicked his opponents around. He began to realise just how powerful he was. And he started to enjoy himself.

'Puny gnomes, vile ogres, you're no match for me!' Alan shouted and sent out a great slime pulse that knocked them all to the ground.

'You're right, duck,' said a voice. 'But I will be.'

Acidic Alan looked down. Standing in front of him was Hagatha Squint having a drink of something yellow in a flask. As he watched, he noticed there was something different about her. She looked gooier. But not gooey and green like him. Gooey and bright yellow . . . yellow like a fresh corn-on-the-cob. She was so yellow that she glowed.

'What do you want, apprentice?' said Alan dismissively.

'Oh, I'm no longer an apprentice,' Hagatha Squint said, 'thanks to my friends, Louis and Pearlin.'

As Alan watched, Hagatha Squint transformed from an apprentice witch into . . . a slime sorcerer! Hagatha felt a wave of happiness and wellbeing flow through her new slimy body. She was a true slime sorcerer, pure and yellow like a zingy, lemon jelly, not green like a big old pile of snot. She was ready for anything!

'NO!' barked Alan. 'I am the only slime sorcerer!' And he fired off a huge flood of green slime at her.

Hagatha held up her arms and created a shield of yellow slime to protect herself.

'My turn!' she said and pointed her finger, firing off a thin blast of yellow slime that poked Alan in his middle.

'Agh!' he cried.

And lo, the battle of the slime sorcerers began.

Which was very epic.

And very exciting.

Especially when all the gnomes and ogres returned to join in the fight.

Along with Mysto with his triple-headed wand.

And Champion Trixie.

And Catalogue.

And Pearlin and Mac n Cheese.

Just take a look for yourself . . .

But which also meant . . .

Alan was too busy to notice Louis and Wurt getting into Clunkalot's inner compartment and clip-clopping into Alan's giant green body.

'Come on Wurt. Let's finish this!'

CHAPTER 54

'We must retrieve Chris the sword,' said Louis. 'Everything depends on it.'

Clunkalot galloped and jumped inside Alan. The slime sorcerer barely noticed. He was too busy fighting everyone else. Clunkie had to lower his extra legs to push himself through the thick gelatinous slime.

'Keep going, Clunkie!' said Louis. 'The sword's over there!'

Clunkalot edged forwards, closer and closer to Chris. At last, they were right in front of it.

'Ready?' said Louis to Wurt.

'Why don't you do it?' said Wurt nervously.

'I'd love to,' said Louis. 'But I'm not sure Chris the sword would work for me. I'm not an ogre. Plus I've already got a sword.'

'But you're a knight,' said Wurt. 'I'm only a squire.'

'Then let's fix that,' said Louis. 'Kneel.'

It wasn't easy as they were crammed inside Clunkalot's inner compartment. But Wurt managed to kneel and Louis tapped him on each shoulder with the flat of his sword, Dave.

'In the name of Squirrel Helm, I give you the right to wield Chris, and the power to meet justice. Arise, Knight Sir Wurt!'

Wurt stood. In one sense, nothing had changed. But in another way, everything had. Wurt had always wanted to become a knight and a hero. And now he was one, with a difficult and dangerous mission to complete. Would he rise to the challenge? Or would he run away screaming, *ah ah ah a giant slimy wizard. I've got to get out of here!*

I THINK I'D GO FOR THE LAST OPTION MYSELF

'You and Clunkie had better go,' said Knight Sir Wurt to Sir Louis. 'I've got a job to do.'

'That's the spirit,' said Louis with a smile.

Then Sir Wurt opened Clunkie's hatch and swam out into the green slimy insides of Alan.

Louis closed the hatch. 'Time to get digging again, Clunkie!'

Clunkalot's hooves turned into shovels and he burrowed into the ground underneath Alan. Dig dig dig!

Meanwhile, Acidic Alan was fighting and flinging and feeling furious. He was extremely annoyed about Hagatha. How had she managed to become a slime sorcerer? Unbelievable! He had never intended to make Hagatha a slime sorcerer like himself. And somehow her yellow slime magic seemed more powerful than his green stuff!

'I must find out how she's become so powerful,' he thought to himself, 'then I can take that power and become even more powerfully powerful with the most powery power ever. Ha ha!'

It was then he noticed something burrowing out of the ground. It was that metal robot horse thing. What was going on? The horse's side hatch opened and there was Knight Sir Louis again.

'YOU! Annoying child,' shouted Alan. 'I bet you're behind all this aren't you?'

'I am, yes,' said Louis. 'Even though I'm just a boy.'

'Yeah,' said Catalogue coming up beside Louis. 'Because this boy and his here chums are way smarter than you. Just cos we're younger than yous don't mean we're stupid.'

'HA! You haven't defeated me yet,' Alan sneered.

'No,' said Louis. 'But we will in three . . . two . . . one . . .'

Alan heard a strange sound from inside his own body.

It sounded like a little wobbly voice saying . . . 'I've got it!'

Louis and Catalogue looked up and saw Wurt finally grabbing the sword Chris inside Alan. Slowly but surely, he swung Chris above his head.

And then in the same wobbly voice he spoke the magic words.

BY THE POWER OF TUMBLIN' KLATTERBANG!

A lightning bolt blasted out of the sky and went straight through Alan until it touched the tip of the stone sword inside him.

The slime around Chris the sword began to turn to stone.

'Uh-oh,' Wurt said. 'Time to go!' And he scrabbled towards the hole that Clunkie had dug.

Slowly but surely, around the sword more and more of Alan's slimy body turned to stone. The slime sorcerer roared with anger and tried to slide away. But he found he couldn't. His whole lower section was now solid and fixed to the ground.

'I'll get you for this!' shouted Alan and he swung his giant slimy arms down to whack Louis.

Louis ran away as fast as he could. Was he going to make it?

Let's hope so. This is supposed be a funny book, not a tragedy.

Alan's gigantic arm swung down –

– and then suddenly stopped.

Alan's arm and the rest of his body had turned completely to stone! His clenched fist was just above Louis' helmet.

'Phew! That was a close one,' said Louis.

And then the cheers went up.

HAROOO!
HOORAY!
WAHOOO!

Catalogue raced over to Louis. 'We gone and did it,' she said.

FINAL SCORE

ACIDIC ALAN **0** **1** TEAM SIR LOUIS

HOORAH!

CHAPTER 55

'We did,' said Louis. 'Though it looks like Castle Sideways is going to be stuck with a very large statue!'

Hagatha Squint oozed over to them. 'I think I can help with that,' she said.

And she muttered some words under her breath.

SLOOPY GLLOOOOPY SQUIP!

She fired yellow slime at the great statue, and it began to rumble and then it collapsed into a pile of sand. Stuck in the sand were two things. A stone sword – Chris. And a man – Baron Alan of Blunder.

He took a deep breath, coughed and then looked around very confused.

'Oh! Ah! What? Where am I?' said Baron Alan. 'What's going on?'

Mysto stepped forward. 'Ho there, Baron. Remember me? Let me fill you in on what you've been up to for the last one thousand years.'

And then . . . well, everyone was rather hungry after all that battling. It was time for a banquet.

CHAPTER 56

Night had fallen. The stars were out. The moon had come too. The sun was a bit annoyed about not being invited, but it was night after all.

There were so many ogres, gnomes and people from across the Many Kingdoms at the celebration banquet that it was decided to have it outside Castle Sideways on the plain.

Knight Sir Louis sat together with Pearlin, Wurt, Catalogue, Trixie, Hagatha and Mysto. King Burt the Not Bad congratulated each of them on a job well done.

BURT MEET WURT.
WURT MEET BURT.

Then it was time for King Burt to take his throne at the top table.

'Er . . . hello everybody,' said Burt rather sheepishly. 'I'd like to apologise for being a total nincompoop. Even more nincompoopish than folks like Jingo Bingo and Felicity Tuckshop. I hereby humbly ask you Louis, please, pretty please, be our champion once again. Will you?'

'Of course, your majesty,' said Louis with a smile.

'HOORAY!' said the crowd.

'Then I declare that you are reinstated as champion of Castle Sideways,' said King Burt. 'And Deputy King once again. And I think you should have a new title for your trouble. I declare that you will become the head of a new league of knights and heroes called, er . . .'

Burt looked around for inspiration. He looked down at the top table which was a particular kind of shape.

'. . . Leader of the Knights of the Slightly Oblong or maybe Oval Table!'

'Thank you, your majesty,' said Louis. 'What a very catchy name.'

And just when everything seemed peachy and Louis was tucking into his second helpings, a flying damsel head burst onto the grassy plain carrying Louis' dad on top of it.

An instant later, Louis leapt onto Clunkalot, shouting, 'Coming, Dad.'

And he flew up into the night to save the day once again.

BACK SOON!
SAVE ME A CORN-ON-THE-COB!

ACKNOWLEDGEMENTS

Thank you to Sir Bella Pearson, Sir Gaia Banks, Sir Lucy Fawcett, Sir Colyn Allsopp, Sir Liz Scott, Sir Ness Wood. Thank you to Evgenia and Lucy for your love and support. And thank you to Louis, now all grown up, for being the original audience of one.

Winners of our
#NameYourKnight Competition

Overall winner:
Knight Sir David the 523rd by Cormac

Highly commended entry:
Knight Sir Jiggly Pig by Ellie and Evelyn

Runners up:
Knight Sir Whiskers by Tom
Knight Sir Flower by Katie
Knight Sir Jeff by Kiko
Knight Sir Night-Night by Gabriela
Knight Sir Gadoces of Mad by Chloe

Have you read the other stories about Knight Sir Louis?

'Sublime daftness on every page!' Jeremy Strong

Knight Sir Louis is the champion knight at Castle Sideways, and the bravest of all knights in all lands. Braver than Knight Sir Colin in the bogs of Wattasmel. Braver than Knight Sir Barbara in the mountains of Itso-Hy. Even braver than Knight Sir Gary from the soggy lands of Tippinitdown.

But Louis is modest. He says he's not brave, but just good at staying calm when everyone else is going completely bonkers.

Along with his trusty mechanical steed, Clunkalot, and mystical sword, Dave, Knight Sir Louis and his friends are sent to do battle with the Damsel of Distresse who is terrorising the land, stealing coins of gold, silver and chocolate. But soon he finds himself dealing with strong enchantments, powerful magic, and evil potatoes . . . all in a normal day for this brave knight. (Just don't mention wasps.) Hooray for Knight Sir Louis!

'A masterclass in silliness!' Gary Northfield

Greg and Myles McLeod are known as The Brothers McLeod for two reasons. The first reason is that they have the same surname. The second reason is that they are brothers. They come up with silly stories together, then Greg draws the pictures and Myles writes the words. They have won things like a BAFTA and make cartoons for people like Disney, the Royal Shakespeare Company and Milkshake!

GUPPY BOOKS

Guppy Books is an independent children's publisher based in Oxford in the UK, publishing exceptional fiction for children of all ages.

Small and responsive, inclusive and communicative, Guppy Books was set up in 2019 and publishes only the very best authors and illustrators from around the world.

From funny illustrated tales for five-year-olds and magical middle-grade stories, to inspiring and thought-provoking novels for young adults, Guppy Books promises to publish something for everyone. If you'd like to know more about our authors and books, go to the Guppy Aquarium on YouTube where you'll find interviews, draw-alongs and all sorts of fun.

Bella Pearson
Publisher

www.guppybooks.co.uk